RIDING ICARUS

Lily Hyde is a British freelance writer and journalist based in Ukraine. She has been covering cultural and social issues in the former Soviet Union for several years, and her journalism and travel writing has been widely published in the international press.

After graduating from university, a childhood fascination with Russian fairy tales led Lily to travel around Eastern Europe where she discovered that fairy tales aren't always true, but the reality is even stranger and more magical. She was inspired to write her first novel, *Riding Icarus*, by the places she has been and the people she has met. She says, "I love listening to people's stories, trying to understand what they dream about, what makes them tick; wondering what our lives would be like if I'd been born in their place and they'd been born in mine."

Books by the same author

Dream Land

Riding
Icarus

LILY HYDE

**WALKER
BOOKS**

First published 2008 by Walker Books Ltd
87 Vauxhall Walk, London SE11 5HJ

2 4 6 8 10 9 7 5 3

Text © 2008 Lily Hyde
Illustrations © 2008 Angela Hogg

This book has been typeset in Sabon

Printed and bound in Great Britain by Clays Ltd, St Ives plc

British Library Cataloguing in Publication Data:
a catalogue record for this book
is available from the British Library

ISBN 978-1-4063-0766-5

www.walkerbooks.co.uk

For Alice, of course

I owe a debt to Max, for village nightmares;
Gareth, who was there for Icarus's first outing;
and the folk tales of Nikolai Gogol,
where I first found the enchanted place.

Chapter 1

Birds whistled. Those were the ones with heads as grey and furry-looking as little mice. There was an endless shushing noise, as if the Dnieper River had slipped the chains of its banks in the night and lay soughing and sighing on the doorstep. The goats in their pen made sleepy bleating sounds. Faintly from the car park above came the banging and scraping of garage doors, the rattle of engines, and the soft squishing of tyres in the sand. The trolleybus wires sang their thin, twanging song.

That was what Masha woke up to every morning. She liked to lie listening before she opened her eyes; she had a running bet with herself to see if she could predict the weather from what it sounded like.

"Sunny but hazy," she said. "Cotton wool sky."

"Get yourself out of bed; the kasha's burning. You and your cotton wool," said Granny, who had no intention of rewarding even correct weather predictions. Granny knew such things as instinctively as cows, or crows.

Masha sighed and opened her eyes. Kasha was buckwheat boiled with butter. Filling and cheap, but boring. Next to it on the table, though, Granny had laid out the remains of Masha's birthday cake. Feeling her stomach rumble, she hopped out of bed.

It was too hazy to be sunny. Less cotton wool than curdled milk. Thunderstorm weather. How do you work out differences like that from sounds? Masha pondered as she slipped out of the open door, which was covered with a curtain against mosquitoes, and into the morning air. Why do the trolleybus wires sing even when there's no wind? she wondered in the privacy of the outside loo.

She returned to her home: Icarus the trolleybus.

Lots of the buses that drove around Ukraine had the name ICARUS written on their fronts, but there was only one trolleybus called Icarus. And only this one trolleybus was home to a little girl called Masha and her very old grandmother.

Icarus had not gone anywhere for a long time. He was parked among meadows and allotments on the very edge of Kiev, by the Dnieper River. With no overhead electric wires to fix onto, the two long springy rods attached to the roof waved in the air like antennae, forever searching for a new source of power on which to drive away. There were no seats inside any more, and in their place were two cosy beds, two chairs and a table, and a little cooker which ran off a gas cylinder. A bookcase was tucked between two windows, and a broom handle strung from the ceiling made a rack for the two occupants to hang up their few clothes. The floor was covered with a strip of red carpet, and embroidered Ukrainian cloths were draped across the windows. This mid-summer morning he was a cheerful, bright home with the birdsong pouring in through the open windows and the wires softly keening, a sound both sad and comforting.

Masha eyed her pile of birthday presents from yesterday as she ate her breakfast. It was a very small pile. Nothing at all from her mother, even now she was ten, into double figures: a one as skinny as she was, a fat zero for a peephole onto the world. "A good round number," Granny had said approvingly, as if it were an achievement to reach ten.

Masha didn't want to think about her mother's missing present. She reached over and pulled a big glossy book out of the pile. It was an encyclopaedia of animals. Uncle Igor had given it to her, but she was sure it was not really from Igor at all but from his wife, Anya. She knew this because she actually liked it – in contrast to Uncle Igor's second present, a hideous pink frilly dress his daughter Anastasia had worn once or twice and then got tired of, or grown out of.

"Planning your travels?" Granny said as Masha opened the book to look through Galapagos, where you could ride on giant turtles; the African jungle, full of sleek patterned snakes dripping from the trees. Then she got to Siberian tigers, and Granny sighed and turned away.

Looking at the picture made Masha ache faintly inside. But it was not a new ache; it was already four years old. Her father had grown up beyond Siberia in Kamchatka, thousands of kilometres away to the east, where the tigers live. He said everything there was twice as big as anywhere else. Plants like daisies and dandelions grew so fast, a little sprout would be towering over your head by next morning. Imagine a dandelion as big as a house! Maybe you could use the seeds as parachutes. She'd never asked Papa about that. Perhaps, now, she never would.

Masha shut the book. She suddenly remembered the dream she'd had last night, when it seemed she had followed a great striped burning tiger through sizzling jungle. No, it hadn't been jungle. It had been a night of hot dim velvet under the trees beside the river. She'd been wearing the frilly dress from Uncle Igor, and trying to swim in the Dnieper in it. Her mother – or maybe it was her father – was waiting on the island, waving a white T-shirt like a flag. But the stupid dress clung tightly to her legs, and when she looked down she saw that the frills had turned into green snakes with cartoon smiles and long lolling tongues. They weren't really scary, but she couldn't swim with them tangled round her knees. The current was pulling her under. She struggled, trying to shout for help, and her mouth filled with water. Her mother wasn't there any more; there was just a big black cauldron with smoke oozing out of it under the oak trees on the island.

Masha felt slightly aggrieved that she'd woken up at this point. Maybe something really exciting had been about to come out of the cauldron. She considered telling Granny about the dream. Granny would probably know what happened next – if she hadn't put the dream into Masha's head in the first place. You never knew with Granny.

There wasn't time to mention it because her best friend, Gena, appeared at the door with his new rollerblades. They went off to the car park by the market to try them out.

Gena lived in Masha's old home, a flat on the seventh floor of a concrete tower block, with green lampshades and a piano. He shared it with his mother, Ira, while his father was away working in England. His father paid the rent, and for presents like rollerblades, and even a summer holiday in England.

"He bought me proper football boots as well as the rollerblades," Gena told Masha proudly. "I quite like having a father in England really."

"One in Kamchatka is better," Masha said quickly, and Gena knew not to argue.

Masha's father didn't pay anything, which was why the flat with the lampshades and the piano had been sacrificed. He had gone away again to Kamchatka four years ago, but this time he hadn't come back. Then Mama's friend Igor had appeared. Igor, who told Masha to call him uncle even though he wasn't, and who had found Mama a job abroad where she could earn lots of money. So Mama had gone to Turkey, leaving Masha with Granny. But when the money Mama promised to send didn't come, and didn't come, and didn't come, it was Igor's idea for them to rent out the flat for some income. Now they lived in the trolleybus, waiting for the little house rich Uncle Igor had promised to build them, of which not one brick had appeared so far.

Masha didn't mind. She loved living inside Icarus. Granny fretted about winter, though, and how they would survive there when it was so cold the little mousy-headed birds keeled over on their branches stone dead, frozen justlikethat.

But winter was ages away. It was summer, and the tarmac was sticky with heat under the rollerblade wheels. They went instead to the river to swim.

"You know, people hardly ever swim in English rivers," said Gena as they cooled off in the brown water. "Everyone says they're too dirty. People really worry about things being dirty, over there."

Gena liked talking about England. It sounded a mad place to Masha. Full of castles and cafés, where everyone ate porridge for breakfast in their red brick houses, each with a square of lawn outside guarded by garden gnomes. "But they don't grow anything in their gardens," Gena said. "Except at Alice's. Her family grow their own strawberries."

Alice was Gena's new friend in England. Masha felt a bit jealous of her. Alice had a piano too, and a creature called a guinea pig that Gena said ate chocolate for breakfast. Her father worked with Gena's, and so Alice even had her very own Cossack outfit to dress up in. Masha felt that was a bit much. Here *she* was living in Ukraine, where those distant romantic figures called Cossacks came from, and she didn't have an outfit to wear. Still, she comforted herself that she was better at Cossack dancing than Alice, because Gena, who went to classes, had been teaching her since Christmas.

"We had so many strawberries this year I got sick and tired of eating them," she said now. "In fact, we fed them to the goats. Even the goats got sick of them."

"I bet your granny put a spell on them to make them grow," Gena said. "I bet she mushed up frogs and snails and dog poo and bats' blood and put it on the plants. Eugh!" he shouted, dancing out of Masha's reach. "Masha's been eating dog poo on her strawberries; no wonder the goats got sick."

Masha kicked out, flattening him under a large wave. They splashed and yelled at each other until a fisherman told them off.

Masha's grandmother was a witch – everyone knew that. Most people, not just Masha, called her Babka, or Granny, Praskovia, and when she had lived in the village people had come from all over to seek her advice. She had moved to Kiev to look after Masha, and now her bunches of herbs hung from Icarus's ceiling, and bundles of soft, dark beeswax candles sat on a shelf next to the icons of Mary and the saints. People still came to see her, sometimes.

Masha could remember having terrible nightmares when she was much younger, about snakes. Worried, her mother had taken her on the long dusty trip to Granny's house in the village. She remembered Granny filling a bowl with gleaming water and pouring wax from a burning candle into it. The wax had bubbled slowly into ballooning shapes that were magically hard and cold when they came out of the water.

Granny had taken out one of the boards that made up the bed next to the stove. She'd told Masha to crawl through the gap seven times. Masha thought with awe about how small she must have been then to fit through the space. She'd slept on that bed for three nights afterwards, and not had a single nightmare. Dream snakes were never scary any more.

She told Gena about last night's snaky dream as they lay on the grass to dry off. The air was so hot and heavy it felt like a blanket over their faces.

"They don't have snakes in England either," Gena said. "They have these things called slow-worms."

"So what?" said Masha. "All worms are slow."

When she came home she was exhausted. They had skated some more, they'd played at being Cossacks fighting the Turks, and practised some dancing. The haze had thickened into dense clouds, but it had got hotter and hotter. Now thunder was growling somewhere in the distance, like a gigantic grumpy tiger complaining all the way away in Kamchatka.

Granny was sharp and fretful. She hustled the goats into their pen, swept the trolleybus floor and tied a couple of curious knots in the corners of the curtains.

"What are those for?" Masha asked. She got no answer, which showed that Granny really was unsettled. "It's only a thunderstorm."

"There's no such thing as only a thunderstorm."

When she thought about it, Masha agreed. Thunderstorms were too huge and amazing to take for granted. They raced across the flat fields of Ukraine every summer like the invading hordes of Mongol Tatars, shining and rumbling and terrible in strength.

Masha settled down on her bed to read the animal encyclopaedia. Outside the windows, the hollyhocks fluttered petals like bright rags and the willow trees tossed and heaved, flashing the silver undersides of their leaves. On the page the striped orange tiger glowed. *The Siberian tiger is the largest member of the cat family in the world*, Masha read. *Specimens have been found measuring over three and a half metres in length*.

Overhead, the trolleybus wires bounced and quivered. The whole bus swayed lightly. How long am I?

wondered Masha. I mean, how tall. One metre five, ten? She was tall for her age, taller than round, fair Gena. But three and a half metres was unimaginably big. Bigger than Uncle Igor. Bigger even than Papa, she thought, with a sudden memory of sitting high, high up on her father's shoulders, looking down haughtily on her kingdom. A tiger that took up the whole world.

She tried to read further but it was suddenly too dark. It was utterly still and close and silent. She fell into a moment of emptiness that stretched on … and on…

Crack! went the thunder, right overhead. It was the sound of a vast backbone breaking in half; it made Masha feel sick. The trolleybus wires were thrumming and swinging. Where was the lightning? Where the rain?

"Granny…" she said nervously. As she watched, Babka Praskovia was suddenly illuminated, like an X-ray, and for a moment Masha could have sworn she saw the delicate shadows of her grandmother's bones, and other dim shapes swimming mysteriously in the whiteness. Then it went dark again.

"Granny…" She opened her mouth to say it, but a huge roar came out: it was the thunder; it was the pain of broken bones; it went on for ever. She could see her grandmother shouting at her, but she could hear nothing. Masha shook her head, shouting back, and Granny seized her arm and began pulling her towards the doorway.

Masha pulled the other way. Granny must be mad, taking her outside! She'd be blinded, she'd be deafened, trampled by the huge paws of the storm. They struggled in the open doorway, yelling at each other and hearing nothing, while the world went once more dazzlingly white.

Then Icarus moved. A sudden, violent lurch forward. Granny tumbled off the step outside, and Masha fell inside. And Icarus, antennae suddenly straining onto an invisible humming wire, drove away into the storm.

Chapter 2

Masha found herself squashed into the small space between the gas cylinder and the bookcase. The floor vibrated beneath her knees and all around was the familiar whining hum of a moving trolleybus. Icarus lurched and staggered as he drove along. Branches whipped the sides with violent cracks and scratches, and a deluge of rain rapped sharp knuckles on the roof.

In the sickening seconds of illumination Masha saw leaves and twigs rushing past the windows, and other things too: what looked like shrieking faces and burning flames. In between the deafening bursts of thunder, the trolleybus hummed like a huge, angry swarm of bees. She covered her ears with her hands and wondered whether she was screaming. She could not hear. The trolleybus racketed and bucketed along, taking her somewhere, all alone into the darkness, away from Granny. She kept remembering Granny's look of utter surprise as she fell into the shaking hollyhocks, and began to cry.

The world jumped horribly from white to black to white to black. A book fell out of the bookcase and hit her on the head, and her tears stopped at once as if a tap had been turned off. What was the point of crying? No one was going to hear her. Not the storm, not Granny, not Icarus. Of course not Icarus; he was a machine, and machines ran on electricity and had drivers. And brakes.

The trolleybus tipped wildly, throwing Masha sprawling across the floor almost to the driver's cabin. In the lightning's flash, she could see clearly that it was empty. She crawled towards it, through a storm of books tumbling from the bookcase. The floor was wet where the rain streamed in through the open windows; her knees were cold and they hurt. She reached up for the handle, the door swung inwards and she fell into the cabin.

She'd been in there before, of course, playing at driving the trolleybus to exciting destinations. It made a good spaceship control room too. It was such a cosy little place, with its high leather seat, its rows of buttons and lights. Now lots of the lights were on, twinkling and flashing madly red and green and yellow. Rain flooded down the windscreen, and as she watched from behind the driver's seat, leaves flattened themselves against the glass and then vanished with a hideous screech.

The humming was louder in here. Brakes! thought Masha. Brakes, brakes, brakes. Where were they? She tried to remember her father driving their old battered car, years ago.

The bouncy seat squeaked as if a fat driver were shifting his bottom in it. Masha thought she saw a boneless white hand glue itself to the outside of the windscreen. It stuck there like a bloodless, rubbery strand of seaweed, long enough for her to see the curling, knife-sharp painted nails. Then it slowly peeled off and disappeared.

Masha screamed. She heard herself this time. Another lurch threw her forward, and lightning illuminated a row of pedals on the floor.

"Brakes, brakes, oh, *please* let them be brakes," Masha sobbed. She grabbed the nearest pedal and pushed it downwards as hard as she could.

Icarus groaned and shuddered. The lightning vanished, and as the humming died away, the trolleybus faltered unhappily – and ground to a halt.

It was so quiet! The rain had stopped; the trolleybus had stopped; the thunder and lightning had ceased as though they had never been. Outside something went *drip … drip … drip* extremely slowly, as if there were all the time in the world for a drop of water to loiter down to the ground.

Masha stayed crouched beneath the driver's seat like a tiny little mouse. She still leant all her weight on the pedal that had stopped the madness. She did not want to let go. She did not want to move. She couldn't stop seeing the hand stuck to the windscreen. Now that she had halted the trolleybus's headlong rush she wanted to carry on, further and further away from whatever lurked outside.

It was thinking of Granny that made her move. Granny tumbling into the hollyhocks, not knowing where Masha and her home had driven off to. Maybe she'd hurt herself when she fell. She was very old, after all; no one knew exactly how old. She wasn't even Masha's grandmother really but her great-grandmother. Maybe she was still lying there on the cold ground.

Slowly, carefully, Masha let go of the pedal. It eased itself upwards with an indulgent sigh, but Icarus remained motionless. The lights on the dashboard were slowly fading. It was not quite dark outside, and the view through the rain-blurred windscreen was reassuringly ordinary: bushes, grass, a scrap of fence. Masha tried to feel brave. She didn't quite succeed, but she did manage to open the cabin door and pass through to the main door, still jammed open. She pulled aside the curtain and jumped out quickly before she had time to get too scared.

The light was gentle and dim. She was standing in a meadow bordered by tall willow trees, through which water glimmered. To one side there seemed to be allotment fences made of the usual leafy willow wands interwoven with all sorts of odds and ends. She didn't know exactly where she was but it looked familiar, as if it was a corner she'd often walked through but never really noticed before. When she looked up, the sky was already clearing to a blue so muted it was almost colourless. She thought she could even pick out a couple of the first evening stars. And Icarus was there behind her, fat and cream and red striped and looking as innocent and comforting as if the terrifying ride had never happened.

No rubbery hands or screaming white faces. Nothing scary. Only she really couldn't work out where she was.

As she tried to decide which way to go, a big lump of tears and fright jammed itself in her chest. It was like a jigsaw put together out of order; she recognized all the pieces but she couldn't quite make sense of them. Trying to swallow the lump down to somewhere more comfortable, she sternly counted off in her mind: river, allotments, meadow, trees. If the river is there and the allotments are here, that means I should go … which way? If the trees are between me and the river, that means…

She was distracted by a noise. A curious slapping sound, like someone beating a carpet perhaps, or jumping up and down doing aerobics. People often came to the riverbank to do their exercises. Young men practising kung fu kicks; fat ladies trying to touch their toes. She knew some of the more regular exercisers quite well. People brought their carpets here too, so they could wash and beat the dust from them. The noise she could hear wasn't frightening; it was as eerily familiar as the woods and the water. She went to find out what it was.

Like everything else that evening, she recognized it immediately. It was just in the wrong place. It was a Cossack, and he was dancing.

Chapter 3

Of course Masha knew who he was. Didn't she have books full of pictures of Cossacks? Hadn't her mother taken her to the theatre to see thunderous Cossack choirs? Couldn't she Cossack dance herself?

That was where Cossacks belonged. On stage, in picture books, in dancing classes. Somewhere way back in the past, when there were feasts and heroes and battles with Tatars and Turks.

This Cossack stamped on the ground with heavy feet in worn boots. He had a moustache as fat as two droopy sausages stuck to his face, and the long top-knot sprouting from the crown of his bald head spun round like the blades of a helicopter, so fast was he whirling and twirling, crouching and leaping. His wide scarlet trousers ballooned out with each rotation; his white shirt was a moony blur in the dimness.

Such dancing! It was fast; it was furious; it was glorious. Masha could almost hear the squealing fiddles, the raging drums, the handclaps pattering faster and faster as round, round, round he went, filling the night with speed and heat and sparks. Still faster, still higher—

And then it all fell apart. Somehow he missed a step, something went wrong, the fiddles broke their strings, the drum exploded, the Cossack stumbled and fell over as the end of his topknot swung round and hit him smack in the eye.

"Damn and blast you! May your eyeballs drop out and be eaten by cockroaches, you stinking pile of horse manure!" roared the Cossack in a voice as huge as half an orchestra.

Masha trembled. Was he shouting at her? But the Cossack did not look in her direction. He sat with his elbows on his knees, wiping the sweat from his face with a hand like a beef steak.

"Cursed ground," he grumbled. "Can't you let an honest Cossack dance in peace?" He shook his fist in the air, and that was when he caught sight of Masha.

"What monstrous object are you?" he rumbled in his enormous voice, heaving himself to his feet and advancing upon her threateningly.

"I'm not a monstrous object; I'm a person," she quavered. His clenched fists looked as large as her head. "I liked your dancing. Why did you stop?" she added in a desperate attempt to make him more friendly.

"I didn't stop – this enchanted place stopped me. The devil, may his tail wrap round his neck and choke him, stopped me," boomed the Cossack. He did, however, unclench his fists. "How did you get here?"

At the thought of explaining about Icarus, Masha's nerve failed her. "I don't know," she said in a small voice, thinking what a stupid answer that was.

But the Cossack's blue eyes grew friendlier by the minute. "That makes two of us," he said, "because I can't say how I came here either. One minute I'm drinking and dancing with my friends by my melon patch; the next, that sneaking cowardly devil has whisked me off here and I can't finish the hopak, may his toenails rot off."

"The devil?"

"Who else but that miserable lump of sheep's offal? Wait till I get my hands on him – I'll tie his ears round his ankles and kick him into the middle of next week."

"The middle of next week," somebody distinctly said behind them.

They both turned round. Beneath the starry sky and the soft shade of the willow trees, nobody was there. Masha realized she'd taken hold of one of the Cossack's big warm hands in fright. She was a bit embarrassed, but he didn't seem to mind.

"What a sly one," he said. "Will the wretch come out into the open? Of course not. A pair of honest Ukrainians like us is enough to scare the tiny wits out of his turnip of a skull."

Silence all round. Maybe the Cossack was right.

"Where in the world, or out of it, are we?" he mused, tugging at the fat moustache which drooped down to his chin. "Where has that interfering slyboots brought us?"

"I sort of know," said Masha. "I mean, I think I recognize it – only I don't quite know where it is."

"That's not very helpful," the Cossack commented.

Masha looked around again, hoping to spot a familiar landmark. She pulled at his hand in excitement.

"Look! Something's over there."

Beneath the trees was a glow of eerie, greenish light. They approached cautiously. It came from a candle standing on a long, raised hump of ground overgrown with ferns. The green-tinged flame stretched itself up tall, then squashed down small and guttering in a non-existent breeze. Then it went out.

It was dark and cold under the trees. The hump of ground looked sinisterly like a grave.

"Do you think someone's buried there?" Masha whispered, clinging to the Cossack's comforting hand.

"Not some*one*, some*thing*," cried her companion. "Buried treasure, that's what – I'll bet my boots and my best bonnet."

"Treasure?"

"Of course. What else would you expect to find in an enchanted place? Let's get digging." He detached his hand from hers and hitched up his trousers – and slapped his forehead with a cry of frustration. "No spade," he groaned. "Have you got a spade?"

"No, but there's one inside Icarus."

"Icarus?"

"The trolleybus," she explained. "It's where I live. He's just over here." She turned round to where she could still dimly see the striped trolleybus sides, black and grey now in the darkness.

There was a click and a hum. The trolleybus head-lights came on, illuminating two thick paths of light through the trees.

"Mind, please, the door is about to close," said the precise, tinny voice of a recorded announcement, like that on the public trolleybuses that drove around the town. Icarus's door scraped shut. "Next stop, Bare

Mountain," Masha thought she heard the voice, muffled now, announce. The hum rose to a whine and the trolleybus trundled away, squeaking as it bounced over the uneven ground.

They stared after it open-mouthed.

"Now how am I going to get home?" wailed Masha. "How will I ever find Granny?"

The Cossack was tugging at his moustache again. "Me a grandfather, and I've never seen anything like that before," he muttered. "The devil's really up to his tricks tonight. And how are we going to mark this spot, hey? I'm damned if I'm going to lose sight of my treasure."

He cast about on the ground until he caught sight of an old log lying under one of the trees.

"X marks the spot," he said cheerfully, dragging the branch over to lie beside the candle.

Masha wrapped her arms around herself to try and stop shivering. "But we don't know where we are," she observed disconsolately, "so how can we find it again?"

"I thought you said you recognized it?"

"Yes, but it's all wrong. Everything's in the wrong place," Masha tried to explain as the tears trickled down her nose. "I know there's the river, and the allotments…"

As she looked about her again, she saw a plump round onion shape outlined against the sky behind the allotments.

"Isn't that the church dome?" she said doubtfully.

"Of course it is!" exclaimed the Cossack. "Who says we're lost? And over there on the other side, above the trees, that's the pole of the deacon's dovecote."

Sure enough, it was, although who the deacon was Masha couldn't imagine; the dovecote had been empty and abandoned as long as she had known it. The sight of the two familiar landmarks was such a relief, she almost forgot about Icarus's mysterious departure.

"Now I know how to get home," she said, sniffing furiously. "It's this way."

"So is my melon patch," said the Cossack. "I wonder how many have been stolen while I've been gone."

"And I wonder how Granny is. I must get back as quick as I can. Oh, please, will you come with me? I don't know if she's all right."

She asked this because now it was quite dark, and the woods were silent and alarming, and the candle on the grave under the trees belonged to some other world than the one she was used to by day. The Cossack, even though she had met him under such strange circumstances, was big and friendly and didn't seem to be frightened of anything. She didn't think she could walk all the way back on her own, and find there – what?

"A young Cossack like you, afraid of the dark?" he said, rather unkindly. "Still, I don't see why we can't step out together, seeing as I'm heading in the same direction. We victims of the devil's little jokes, may he be afflicted with corns, wind and nose pimples, ought to stick together." He scratched his stomach and yawned hugely. "Come on then, young fellow. What's this about your grandmother?"

Chapter 4

Gena, making his way down the sandy bank that led to the allotments and the river, came upon a scene of devastation. In the clear hot sunlight he had almost forgotten the storm of last night, which had left no mark on the high concrete tower block where he lived. But here the world was more impressionable. Fences were torn down, bushes flattened, leaves drowned in shining blue puddles and sand rucked up into drifts and ridges. A few allotment owners in shorts and bikinis picked their way among the debris, lamenting.

Gena began to worry how Masha and her grandmother had survived the storm. He hurried on, his feet sinking and sliding in the sand, to where their old trolleybus was beached beneath the silver-green willow trees.

There was a gleaming black Mercedes parked in the sunlight, its engine purring and all its dark tinted windows reflecting the sun dazzlingly. What a beautiful car! The shadows cast on its sides were satiny red and purple, and heat bounced off it in visible shimmers.

Gena cupped his hands to peek through a window. Catching sight of his round face peering in, the driver inside waved irritably and mouthed through the glass, "Go away."

Gena backed off reluctantly. The car belonged to Masha's rich Uncle Igor, and Gena had long held a sneaking hope that one day he'd get to sit inside on its sleek upholstery.

There was no sign of Igor today. The car sat in alien splendour on the yellow sand, immaculate amid the chaos. One of the willow trees had been uprooted and lay smashed against the bank. The tall hollyhocks were stretched out in a spatter of pink and red petals, like slaughtered soldiers, and the shattered raspberry canes were half buried in leaves and squashed fruit. One of the goats was busily licking up raspberry purée.

Gena was at Icarus's door before he realized there was no door. He stopped, puzzled. Everything looked different after the storm. He picked his way round the battered trolleybus to the entrance on the other side, and the wires overhead creaked a little.

Masha was inside, surrounded by scattered books and forks and spoons. She was packing up clothes in a plastic bag.

"Hi," said Gena. "It's me. Wow, what a storm! What happened to your raspberries?"

Masha looked terrible. She had big dark rings under her eyes and her cheeks were all puffy as if she had been crying.

"What's up?" he asked uncertainly.

"Oh, Gena," she said in a trembling voice, "I'm so

glad you're here. Granny's in hospital and everything's a mess and I've got to take her some stuff. Please come with me. I don't know if she's all right, I don't know what's the matter with Icarus and I don't know where I'm going to live and everything's *awful*."

She did not manage to tell him all that had happened until much later. First they went to the hospital, chauffeured by Uncle Igor's driver, who kept his mirrored sunglasses on and lit a cigarette so that smoke curled and billowed in the air-conditioned interior of the Mercedes. Gena found it quite disappointing. He couldn't enjoy the bouncy seats and the purring smoothness of the ride with Masha hunched up next to him all tense and nervous, clutching the bag of her grandmother's things and refusing to talk because *he* – she indicated the supercilious driver lurking behind his shades – would hear.

At the hospital the nurse would not allow them in to see Babka Praskovia. They left the forlorn bag with a pair of slippers in it, and a toothbrush that Granny never used, and a nightdress she never wore.

"The driver's supposed to take me to Uncle Igor's but I really don't want to go. Please can I come back with you instead?" Masha whispered. "Will your mother mind?"

"Why don't you want to go to Igor's?" If Gena had known someone with a brand new limited edition Mercedes, he'd have jumped at the chance to see where he lived. A few years ago, it was impossible for anyone in Ukraine to own such a car; even now there were very few people rich enough.

Masha only glared at him miserably, so he added, "All right, I'm sure Mama won't mind."

Masha leant forward. "Please take Gena home first," she said to the driver, adding the address in a small voice.

The driver merely shrugged, but he took them as asked to the flat. Gena hoped that everyone would notice him getting out of the fabulous car, and was pleased to see that there were plenty of old ladies sitting on the benches by the entrance, enjoying the sunshine and watching with the appropriate level of interest.

Masha scrambled out of the car too. "I'm staying here," she said quickly, and slammed the door.

The driver's door opened and he looked as if he was going to step out after her. But then Gena got the distinct impression that his gaze, hidden behind the sunglasses, took in the old ladies on the benches watching what was going on with completely undisguised curiosity. Without a word the driver closed the door and the car slid away.

Gena's mother Ira was wonderfully comforting. She hugged Masha lots of times, and gave them both cups of sweet tea and raspberries with cream. She would call Igor and organize everything so that Masha could stay, she said, and she promised to phone the hospital to find out when they could visit Granny.

All the stiffness and tension finally went out of Masha, and she collapsed onto the divan and told Gena the whole story. She told him about the storm and the ride, the candle on the grave, and how she had come back in the chill, whispering night to find Icarus the trolleybus parked where he had always been, the door open, and Granny lying still and silent on the muddy ground. Masha had run to the car park where the nightwatchman sat up in his cabin, and he had called an ambulance and dosed her with powerful coffee and condensed milk. She had waited the interminable time until the ambulance came, and white-coated strangers lifted Babka Praskovia inside, taking Masha along too to the hot, wailing, noisome hospital. Granny had been wheeled off to a ward and Masha, forgotten, had curled up to sleep in a corner. When they had finally remembered her and asked about relatives, the only person she could think of had been Uncle Igor.

"Why didn't you call me?" asked Gena.

"They said it had to be a relative," Masha said. She wished that she had called Gena and his mother instead.

"He's not your relative," Gena objected.

"No. But he's supposed to help. Mama promised when she went away that he would," Masha said fiercely. "He's horrible. He only sent his driver."

It was hard reliving the storm and the night while sitting here on cushions, the sun slanting in through the windows and drawing out a dim, baking smell from the furniture. Especially the Cossack – that was almost the strangest part of the adventure. Their walk home together along the mosquito-humming, black lapping river seemed absolutely dreamlike. He had kept on calling her a boy, until she became too embarrassed to correct him. He told her about his grandsons who helped look after his melon patch, making sure no one stole any melons while he was gone. He told her another story about the devil that made her scalp tingle, although his voice seemed to slither into the river and emerge again all smooth and wet and quiet as she walked along, sleepier and sleepier, the words washing into one ear and trickling out of the other...

When they had arrived back at the trolleybus he had taken charge at once, looking over her grandmother gently, telling Masha to run for help, reassuring her that Granny would be all right. Yet when the ambulance came, red light circling in the darkness, she'd forgotten him in all the confusion. He must have disappeared sometime when she'd been climbing into the back, because when she remembered and looked out to say thank you, there had been no one there.

There was a silence when she finished.

"Wow," said Gena eventually.

"Really?" he added.

"I mean ... is that all really *true*?" he asked.

Masha threw a cushion at him. "What do you mean, is it true?" she shouted. "Do you think I made all that up? Look at Granny and the trolleybus and everything! It was the scariest night of my life; of course it's true."

"But – it's just not possible." Gena was trying to believe as hard as he could, but nothing he knew about trolleybuses and thunderstorms had ever given him the idea that such a wild ride could happen.

"I suppose Icarus got struck by lightning," he said at last doubtfully, "and that's where he got the electricity from to drive away. But how did he start up again? I'm sorry Masha, but how come he's back in the same place now? You've got to admit that's more than weird."

Masha bounced on the divan with rage. "Idiot! Moron! You've been there. He isn't in the same place.

He's parked the other way round!"

Gena frowned, considering. This morning, when he'd gone to the door of the trolleybus, it hadn't been in its usual place. Was Masha right, and Icarus had turned round? The door was now on the other side, facing the bank. But then he wasn't entirely sure he could remember where it had been before. It was all very confusing, especially with Masha glaring at him like that.

"What's all the shouting about?" Gena's mother came into the room. "Why, what big eyes on the pair of you," she commented. "I've just come off the phone to Igor."

"What did he say?" Masha clutched a cushion anxiously.

"Well, he was somewhat surprised you didn't go back to his house with the driver. Quite put out, in fact." Ira seemed rather put out – and a little puzzled – herself. "However, he's going to keep in touch, and he says he will contact the hospital. I called there too, and we can go and visit tomorrow, so there's something to look forward to."

Chapter 5

Lying in bed in Gena's flat was familiar yet utterly strange. This had been Masha's own room once. Now Gena's grandfather lived here in winter, and all summer, when the old man moved to the dacha, it was empty and closed up. It was her old bed she was lying in, but without the pillowcase and quilt cover printed with Olympic bears that she'd slept with as long as she could remember; those were in the trolleybus now.

The room had a slightly stuffy smell and felt very inhabited with bits of her past. A little, six-year-old, eight-year-old Masha seemed to have crept out – from where? From under the bed, perhaps – and was lying in this familiar bed, missing her papa with urgent misery because he had only just gone away; wondering where Mama was, gone to work in that far-sounding sunny place called Turkey, and hating her for not coming back.

On top of those six-year-old and eight-year-old aches were the new ones, an extra skin of the ten-year-old Masha lying in the dark with a strange silence in her ears. Here was no sound of the river whispering, no goats snorting and dreamily bleating. No Granny heartily snoring, because Granny was lying in hospital with her eyes closed, looking very small and unrecognizable under the thin hospital sheets, not snoring at all because of whatever the cross nurses and the tired, brusque doctors had done to her.

Masha felt the terrible tears begin to trickle down her cheeks, lots of them, from four years ago, from two years, from yesterday, from today. She had nobody left, not even Gena, who didn't believe her so they'd quarrelled. Trying not to cry made her cry all the more. She desperately didn't want anyone to hear, so she stuffed her head under the sheets.

She dreamt she was down by the river. She was home, the sky shone like glass and the grass was warm under her bare feet. Beside her the goat kid was pushing its tickly twitching nose into her hand. She rubbed its nubs of horns, and thought how much the black slits in its yellow eyes looked like the money slots in a piggy bank.

"Bah," said the little goat reprovingly.

Masha realized that they really were money slots, and wondered what she could put in them. She didn't have any money, not a kopek. She picked off one of her fingernails instead; it came away quite easily and was round like a thin pearly coin. She carefully posted it through the slot.

"Don't be confused by the new calendar, Masha," the kid said. "I know they tell you your birthday is on midsummer's eve, so you've already had it and now it's too late. But don't you believe it. Like all

Ukrainians, you've got two birthdays. There are two midsummers, and the important one is coming up. You'll get your present then, if you remember to look for it. The devil will try to trick you, so keep your wits about you. And there are people here who'll help you find your birthday present, your heart's desire."

"But when's my second birthday?" cried Masha.

"I told you: midsummer's eve. Don't forget."

"And what's my present?"

"Time's up," the kid said, blinking. "Baaaa." It wandered away nibbling the grass, bleating thoughtfully to itself. It was dazzlingly white against the riverbank. Masha had never seen such gloriously bright colours, the flashing jewelled blue of the water, the grass a dense, delicious green. And there, a sudden splash of cherry red, up in the tree, but not a bunch of cherries. The toe of a red boot.

"Who's that?" called Masha.

"Me," said the boot. Or more accurately, the wide satin green trouser legs; to be more precise, the white embroidered shirt; in fact, a whole little Cossack girl sitting swinging in the tree and, yes, eating cherries.

"Who are you?" asked Masha, sitting in the tree too, which bounced comfortably in the breeze.

"I'm here to help you, that's who," said the little Cossack girl. "You're going to need me, I knew that as soon as I heard you crying."

"How could you hear me crying?"

"You woke me up. You sounded sad."

"I was," said Masha. "But I'm not any more, now I've got my second birthday to look forward to."

"Lucky thing," said the Cossack girl enviously. "I only get one birthday."

"You can share mine," said Masha, and the girl smiled happily. "We'll find out when it is together."

"And find your present together. Is it a deal?"

"It's a deal."

Masha leant forward to shake hands with her new friend. At that moment she tumbled out of the tree, right into the room that had once been hers, just in time to see Gena's mother come in to open the curtains and let in the morning sunshine.

Chapter 6

How much better life looked in the morning (once she'd checked her fingertips, that is: all ten nails present and correct). The sun beamed down with cheerful, innocent clarity; there were little pancakes with jam and sour cream for breakfast; and Gena had forgotten they were arguing and let her borrow his rollerblades. Masha zoomed breezily down the road past the market and car parks and garages until the rollerblade wheels bogged down in the sandy bank that led to the allotments and the trolleybus. It was a good thing the sand was there, actually, as she hadn't worked out how to stop yet.

As she let out the goats and tethered them to their metal stakes, she eyed the kid suspiciously, thinking about last night. Dreams, she knew quite well from Granny, were to be taken seriously.

"Two birthdays," she mused. "And a present. What was that all about, kiddy?"

The money slots in its eyes were black and mysterious,

but the kid just nibbled at the hem of her shorts and then skipped off in search of something juicier.

Tied to the door of the trolleybus was a woven Cossack belt, pink and orange and red with long tassels. It hadn't been there the evening before, when she had come down with Gena's mother to collect a few things and ask the car park nightwatchman to keep an eye on the place. Who did it belong to? The big fat dancing Cossack? Or her friend, the little Cossack girl in her dream? Masha untied the belt and wrapped it round her waist. It went round lots of times, and the tasselled ends dangled down and tickled her knees.

On the way back, she called in at the car park. Fyodor Ivanovich the nightwatchman was sitting up in his cabin, yawning and drinking coffee. He was a good friend of Granny's and Masha's, and he cheered as she speeded in on the rollerblades and had to grab hold of the gate to stop herself.

"You'll put me out of a job," he said. "Who needs a car when you've got those things? How's your grandmother?"

"I don't know; I'm going to see her today. Fyodor Ivanovich," Masha went on hurriedly, "did you see anything strange happen with our trolleybus on the night of the storm?"

"The strangest thing I saw was you coming up here for help, pale as a *rusalka* fleeing from the lightning on the river," he said. "What a state you were in! That was quite a storm. Seemed to have more than just wind and rain in it; seemed to have … I don't know, ghosts…" He shook off a slightly troubled look. "Anyone could have stolen a car from right under my nose that night if they'd wanted to."

Or a trolleybus, Masha thought. "And what about last night? Did anyone go near Icarus? A Cossack, for instance."

"A Cossack? There aren't many of those around, these days. No, there wasn't a soul," he assured her. "I heard one of your goats bleating away, but that's all."

Mysterious indeed. Masha sped back to the flat pursued by a hundred questions.

Perhaps Gena's mother could answer some of them.

"Ira," she asked, "who are Cossacks, exactly?"

Ira had yellow hair like Gena's, but in big bubbly curls, and she wore a lot of green eyeshadow. She and Masha's mother had shared a room in the hostel when they'd both been students, and become fast friends. Masha had known her as long as she could remember.

"Well now, you a Ukrainian and you don't know who Cossacks are!" Ira chided. "Cossacks were escaped serfs, or adventurers, or soldiers – all sorts of people who ran away to live freely in the Ukrainian steppe, back in the days when there were no trees or villages, just grass stretching as far as you could see. Later they established a centre for men and boys called the Setch, on an island in the Dnieper River, and fought against Turkey and the Ottoman slave raids on Ukraine. They had their own government, their own army, their own stories and songs and dances. Does that answer your question?"

"I think so," Masha said, rather sadly. She was thinking of her own mother's stories about history. Back when they had been a family, Mama had sometimes described the landscapes and songs and battles of Ukraine's past so vividly that Masha could almost see and hear them happening.

"But when was this?" she persisted. "Are there Cossacks now?"

Ira looked puzzled. "I'm a history teacher; I can tell you about four hundred years ago, but now? It depends on what you mean by Cossack, I suppose. There are descendants of Cossacks. There are dancers and singers. But historically speaking the Cossacks were gradually incorporated into the Russian army by Catherine the Great, and lost any rights and privileges over the years until they were little more than mercenaries."

That was too technical to be relevant. Masha went back to a more interesting-sounding bit.

"What do you mean, a centre for men and boys?"

"Well, the Cossacks didn't let women and girls share their fighting and drinking and dancing. None were allowed into the Setch. Really there's no such thing as a female Cossack."

Rubbish! thought Masha indignantly. What about her dream friend, the little Cossack girl? And couldn't she herself Cossack dance just as well as Gena?

"Have you seen this?" she asked, tickling the back of Ira's hand with the tassels of the Cossack belt she'd found.

"Now isn't that beautiful!" said Ira admiringly. "Was that a present from your granny?"

"It's a present from a Cossack. A *girl* Cossack."

Gena's mother laughed. "I'm glad to hear it."

The mention of presents brought Masha to her next question.

"Is it true that Ukrainians have two birthdays?"

"Why, do you want another already?" teased Ira. "You've only just had the last one. No, my dear, as far as I know, little Ukrainian girls, like the rest of the world, only have one day a year for presents and birthday cake."

"What about Ukrainian boys?" asked Gena, who had come in to hear the last question.

"Little Ukrainian boys don't deserve any birthday at all until they learn not to bring in lots of dirt on their shoes," replied Ira smartly. "Go and clear it up, now."

That was a disappointing end to a promising conversation, Masha thought. Why did some grown-ups always bring the subject back to dirt, dirt, dirt? Really, sometimes she thought she was better off without any parents at all.

"Why were you asking about birthdays?" Gena said later as they sat by the river again. The sun blazed down and the inexhaustible crickets spun out and reeled in, spun and reeled in the sound of heat steadily rising. On the island, the round-topped oak trees looked very dense and dark green across the glittering water.

Masha glanced sideways at him. "I'm not sure I'm going to tell you."

"Oh, go on. Are you still angry because I didn't believe you? Well, I've changed my mind. I do now."

"*I* don't believe *you*. You're just saying that so I'll tell you why I was asking."

It was too hot to argue. "Oh, go on, Masha," whined Gena, lying flat on his back and squinting at the smooth blue of the sky through his eyelashes. "I promise I'll believe anything you ever say ever again."

"OK." Masha sat up, inspired. "I'm the cleverest, most intelligent, super-duper interesting, beautiful person in the whole world."

"I believe you," said Gena promptly, shutting his eyes.

"And you're the smelliest, stupidest, fattest blob in the universe."

"I believe you," murmured Gena, looking at the warm rosy red inside his eyelids, and the purple shapes that swam slowly across them like fish, like whales.

Masha had won that game so absolutely that there wasn't much left to say, except tell him.

"I heard somewhere – well, someone told me – that I've got another birthday. In fact, they told me that all Ukrainians have two birthdays. You know mine is on midsummer's eve, so I've already had it. But there are two midsummers, and the second one is coming up. I'll have my second birthday then, and they said I'd get a present." My heart's desire, she thought. But she didn't tell that to Gena.

"Who said?"

"Someone."

The purple whales were joined by luminous stars, exploding silently and re-forming and exploding again. A little shining fish of memory stirred, grew, burst brilliantly.

"But there *are* two midsummers," said Gena slowly, opening his eyes. The world around him was coldly, palely coloured now, all washed-out greens and blues. "Like there are two Christmases and two Easters. Alice told me."

"I know, in England they have Christmas two weeks before we do, and Easter's different. But that's just because they've got different Churches from us."

"No, it's weirder than that." The colours had

deepened, warmed themselves. Gena wondered why he'd thought they were so bleached and wintry bright a moment ago. "It's because there are two calendars, I think."

"Eh?"

"It's very complicated. There was an old calendar, but there were too many days in it for how long the year was. Something like that. So all the dates in this old calendar got more and more behind the real date."

Masha stared at him. "I don't get it."

"How many days are there in a year?"

"Everyone knows that: three hundred and sixty-five," she answered impatiently. "Except leap years, then there are three hundred and sixty-six."

"OK. So imagine there are three hundred and sixty-six days in *every* year here. That means our year is a day longer than in England."

"And what?"

"Think about it. The first year, we have Christmas on the same day. But when it's their new year we have another day to go. So *our* new year, January the first, is already *their* January the second. The second year, because our year is a day longer, our Christmas is a day after theirs."

"Mmm." Masha was doubtful.

"And the year after, we are two days behind. Then three, four, until we're way behind England." Gena had sat up and was frowning in concentration. "It didn't happen quite like that really. I'll look it up properly when I get home. But anyway, that's why there are two Christmases and two Easters, and I guess two midsummers."

Masha selected a blade of grass, stretched it carefully between her thumbs and forefingers and blew a long derisive squeak.

"It's true!" Gena objected huffily.

"I'm not disbelieving you," Masha replied. "I'm just showing my amazement."

She blew again, and the shrill blast echoed across the still, blazing water into the shadows of the oaks beyond. A moment later, several black crows exploded out of the trees, cawing loudly, and flew straight over the river towards them. The birds settled in the willow tree behind the two children. They bobbed and wobbled in the slender branches, fidgeting on their big feet, cawing and making strange popping noises, just like corks being drawn from bottles.

"Shh," Gena said to them nervously. "Go and sit somewhere else."

"Look over there," said Masha. "Smoke."

A thin blue line ascended vertically into the air from amid the oak trees on the island. It reached a certain height and then levelled off and hung in a curious flat pancake.

"It's coming from a cauldron, isn't it?"

Gena shaded his eyes to peer across. There did seem to be something bulbous and black under the trees, but he couldn't make out what it was.

"If only we had a boat!" Masha exclaimed, thumping the ground in frustration.

"Why? It's probably just someone cooking shashlik."

But it's exactly like in my dream, Masha thought. She looked for her mother over there, waving a white flag. But she could see nothing, only the fine pencil line of smoke.

Gena gave her a friendly push. "Let's move. These crows are starting to annoy me."

Chapter 7

Masha led Gena along the path between the allotments and the river. The meadow grass was thick with flowers and stood higher than their shoulders. Dozens of tiny grasshoppers pinged out of it as they passed.

A bunch of crows followed them, hopping and flapping and cawing close behind like a gang of irritating little children.

"Where are we going?" asked Gena. The crows were really getting on his nerves.

Masha was in two minds whether to tell him or not. But then, she reflected, he'd told her something very interesting, if unlikely, about her possible two birthdays. It was time to relent. "I'm looking for the place I went to in Icarus. I know it's around here somewhere. It's where you can see the church dome on one side and the dovecote pole on the other."

"OK," Gena was quite excited. After all, it was fun to believe in night-time rides and mysterious buried treasure. He followed her happily, only occasionally stopping to throw lumps of crumbly dry earth at the crows.

The faded blue onion dome of the church was soon visible, peeping through the trees on their right. They went on more slowly, looking out for the pole of the dovecote on the left.

"Got it," said Gena as the pole came into sight, all that showed above the trees of the little wooden hut on its one leg. "So do you recognize the place yet?"

"Bother," said Masha crossly. "Now we can't see the church. We'll have to go back."

They retraced their steps, the crows ahead of them flapping like old bin bags. The church came into view again.

"Now we can't see the dovecote," Masha said, exasperated. "It must be a bit further back again."

They trekked up and down, up and down, in the heat. They tried going nearer the river, and nearer the allotments. The fact was, as the crows seemed to derisively remark, that from nowhere could they see the church and the dovecote at the same time.

"But that's impossible!" Masha was close to tears of annoyance. "It *has* to be here."

Impossible but true. A few steps one way, and the church peeked between the trees. A metre or two the other way, there poked the dovecote. The place where they were both visible simply did not exist.

"Caw! Caw! Ha ha ha!" said the crows.

Gena stopped. "Are you *sure* you came here last night?" He was beginning to doubt Masha's whole story again. The crows' cawing was making his head ring, and it was far too hot to be searching for a place she'd probably just dreamt of. He sat down, and the high grasses towered above his head, enclosing him in a striped pinky-green tent.

"Of course I'm sure!" Masha snapped. But after a moment, she sat down beside him.

"Of course! Caw haw haw!" the crows said in mocking satisfaction, and flapped away.

It was suddenly very quiet in their cage of grass and sunlight. Gena leant his chin on his pulled-up knees, watching a beetle like a shiny, bright blue bead crawl across his toes and onto Masha's. It looked like hard work: each toe a mountain, each space between them a vast ravine. It was exhausting just to watch. And here was an orange butterfly drifting down as if to land on Masha's sandal, and then fluttering away again like a dream of freedom…

Gena glanced up after it – and found himself staring straight into a round, red face with a straw-coloured moustache plastered to it and an outraged expression.

"What are you trying to do – trip me up? Hiding in the grass like a couple of partridges. Honest to God, it's a good thing I didn't bag you for supper!"

"What?" Gena scrambled to his feet in confusion.

But Masha knew exactly who it was. "Hello, Mr Cossack!" she cried.

"Well, if it isn't my fellow adventurer," he exclaimed, his little blue eyes twinkling at her. "Good lad! But where's your spade?"

"Spade?"

"Haven't you come back to look for the treasure?"

"Of course we have!"

Masha jumped up, triumphant. Now Gena would have to believe her story. Here he stood, large as life, a huge fat Cossack with shiny cheeks and a moustache drooping down to his chin. His topknot was hidden under a fraying straw hat, his enormous yellowish feet were bare beneath the folds of his vast red trousers, and he carried a spade over his shoulder.

"You're a brave young lad to come back," he said to Masha. "Doesn't look so scary in sunlight, though, does it? And I see you've brought reserves."

"Why are you calling her a lad?" Gena burst in. "She's a girl."

Masha blushed. "Of course I am," she said crossly. "I'm Masha."

The Cossack goggled at her. "A girl?"

"My name's Masha," she repeated, "and this is my friend Gena. What's your name, please?"

"Nechipor Prokopovich Golokopytenko," the Cossack replied, still staring. "But you can call me Nechipor," he added, noticing them struggling to digest this mouthful. He started to laugh. "Well, bless my soul. If you were a granddaughter of mine, I'd lambast you for trotting around the countryside in that get-up. And in the middle of the night too! You didn't run away, though. A little snip of a girl like you, and you didn't run away. We'll have to call you an honorary Cossack, bless my buttons." And he laughed so much his fat belly quaked.

"What's so funny?" demanded Masha indignantly. "I'm not a little snip." She felt herself glowing pink and thought she might well lose her temper in a minute. "I bet you haven't managed to find the place either, have you?" she said rudely.

"You bet right," Nechipor answered, still chuckling. "You've a mighty forward way of asking, but since old goat-foot himself has put you in my path I'll forbear to mention it. What a joke. Oh, he's a sly one, the horrible hairy old pig-face."

Gena hadn't understood most of this. "Are you looking for the same place, with the grave and the candle, er, Nechipor?"

"Of course I am; I want my treasure! But I'm blowed if I can find it. Up and down, up and down, all the lifelong afternoon, and nothing to show for it but sore heels."

"Exactly!" Masha burst out. "There's nowhere you can see the church and the dovecote at the same time."

"It's a real piece of trickery," Nechipor agreed. "Oh, what a monster, that stinking pile of goat's droppings, may his teeth fall out and his bum be covered in boils."

"Who?" asked Gena, confused.

"The devil, of course," said Masha. "May his ears be bitten by a million mosquitoes."

"Good la— Good girl," said Nechipor approvingly. "I'll tell you, though, you young ones, I've had it for today. This heat's enough to send a fellow barking mad. I'm heading back to my melon patch. You can come with me if you like."

It wasn't often you met someone as loud, as brightly coloured, as puzzling and funny and scary as Nechipor. "Yes, please," they both replied at once.

Nechipor's melon field was deep in the patchwork of allotments that covered the low, sandy ground between the garages and the river. Masha thought she knew the maze of paths pretty well, but she was certain she'd never walked past Nechipor's plot before. The fence was made of sprouting willow wands, wound round with the curly-wurly tendrils of morning glory.

"You should see the flowers in the morning," boomed the Cossack. "Such blue! Blue as Our Lady's gown; you never saw anything like it."

There were raspberries and gooseberries and blackcurrants and redcurrants, which Nechipor offered them in liberal handfuls, but most of the plot was given over to low, creeping marrow and melon plants. Some of the stripy marrows were as long as Masha's arm, but the watermelons were still small, hard green balls. A ramshackle shelter in one corner, built out of all sorts of rubbish, stood over a huge, sagging iron bedstead heaped with blankets and old cushions.

"Do you sleep here?" asked Gena.

"Of course I do. If I didn't the birds and any old thieving vermin would have the lot. And as for the watermelons, they're as much bother as children – need to be covered up from too much sun, turned so they ripen evenly. Honest to God, I think I've spent more time mollycoddling my melons than I ever did my sons and daughters. The thing is, you never know how your children are going to turn out; whatever you want, they want the opposite, the contumacious creatures. But melons now." He folded his hands on his big belly and his moustache twitched in a benign smile. "Give your melons a little care and they'll grow as plump and sweet and juicy as you like." He smacked his lips. "That one there, that's a Turkish melon. Curved like a ram's horn when it's grown. No one grows them but me."

Masha stared at the plant with its blaring trumpet

yellow flowers. "Perhaps my mama's eating melons like that right now," she said wistfully. "She's in Turkey," she explained to the Cossack.

To her surprise, his moustache bristled fiercely and his hand flew to his belt, where, Gena had already noted, he carried a big knife in a leather scabbard.

"In that godforsaken country, that nest of vermin?" he roared. "Carried off, was she, by God; kidnapped by those marauding sons of dogs?"

"Not exactly," said Masha cautiously. "She went there to work."

"Work? That's right, they make slaves of our free-born Cossack maids, steal them from our hearths by night, by stealth, can't fight like men, the cowardly dogs. Oh, that they should enslave our mothers and sisters, our daughters. My blood boils; my Cossack heart burns for action, for revenge!" And he smacked his chest resoundingly with his clenched fist.

Gena and Masha stared open-mouthed. Nechipor looked down at Masha, and his expression softened. "Well, poor little one," he said awkwardly. "And what about your grandmother? Recovered, has she, after your wagon knocked her over like that?"

"Trolleybus," Masha corrected absently. "Granny!" In the excitement of meeting the Cossack again, she'd actually forgotten about Granny. "We're going to see her today. In fact, we should go right now. Come on, Gena."

"But I haven't shown you the place yet, where I was dancing when old bony-knees snatched me off heaven knows where— "

"May his teeth all fall out next time he tries to eat *vareniky*," Masha put in.

"Couldn't have put it better myself," said Nechipor. "Come back soon, young fellows – er, both of you, and I'll show you the cursed spot."

Chapter 8

But they didn't get to see Granny. The nurse at the entrance to the ward, one Masha didn't recognize, closed the door firmly in their faces.

"No visitors," she said. "Doctor's orders."

"But what's wrong with her?" asked Gena's mother. "Can't the doctor talk to us at least?"

"Why can't we see her?" Masha added. "They told us on the phone that we could."

"She's a very old lady," said the nurse. "We have to run a lot of tests. And until we have the results, she can't be disturbed. The doctor's busy; come back next week if you want to talk to him."

"Next week!" exclaimed Ira indignantly. "Now listen to me. This little girl has a right to see her grandmother—"

"You listen to me," the nurse interrupted, her fat cheeks quivering with anger. "We are highly trained medical staff; do you think we don't know what's best for our patients? Either you let us do what's proper or we'll turn her out on the streets, and believe me she's in no fit state for that. If you want her to get medical attention, you leave her with us. Now, did you bring anything with you?"

Ira, her mouth set in a hard line, handed over the bag of fruit and cheese and biscuits they had brought. "When can we see Praskovia Matveyivna?"

"Come back next Friday." The nurse was shamelessly inspecting the food package. "Is this all?"

"How do we know you'll give them to her?" demanded Masha, clutching the bunch of flowers she and Gena had picked.

"Well, little girl, I hope you aren't suggesting they won't get to your grandmother," the nurse replied grimly. "I'm sure you want the old woman to receive the best care possible."

"Of course we do," said Ira hurriedly as Masha opened her mouth to ask the nurse what she meant. "Please tell Praskovia Matveyivna we called, and we will be back next Friday. I hope the doctor can see us then and tell us what's wrong."

"Don't we all hope that," the nurse retorted. She took the flowers from Masha's unwilling hand and folded her arms over the front of her grubby white coat, staring at them until Ira turned away.

"What did she mean?" Masha insisted as they squeaked down the long, dingy hospital corridors. "Why did you give in to her like that?"

"Hush, Masha," said Ira tiredly. "What can we do? If they refuse to keep her here, we can't afford to take her anywhere else. We have to do what they say."

"But why wouldn't they tell us what's wrong?" Masha's voice was small. "Do you think – is Granny really ill, do you think? Is that why we couldn't see her?"

"Oh come now, Masha." Ira put her arm around Masha's shoulders. "I'm sure she's all right. The doctor probably didn't have any time today, that's all. And it's true, your granny is a very old lady. I expect they want to keep her in for a while for check-ups. Don't worry."

"I bet she won't give Granny the flowers or the food," said Masha. "The horrible old pig."

"Don't be rude," Ira said in her schoolteacher voice. They scrunched down the gravel path towards the gates, and she turned to them with a bright smile. "Children, how about ice creams? You stay here and I'll get some. What do you want?"

"Chocolate," said Gena.

"Vanilla," said Masha.

"All right. Back in a minute."

Ira set off down the street. Gena sat on the kerb to wait, but after a moment Masha turned back in through the hospital gates.

"Where are you going?" Gena demanded.

"I'm going to try and find the window of Granny's room. Maybe if we shout she'll hear us. Coming?"

They ran across the dry, scrubby lawns and along by the peeling hospital walls. It was hard to work out where they had been, but Masha thought it was round the corner, and she knew it was on the first floor. A few windows were open, greyish curtains flapping out of them.

"Granny!" called Masha softly. "Granny!"

"Babka Praskovia!" Gena called, even more softly. "What if the nurse hears?" he whispered to Masha.

"You heard what she said. They might turn your granny out."

There was no sign of anyone at the windows.

"I suppose so," Masha said reluctantly. "Anyway, maybe Granny's asleep."

They turned back the way they had come. Then came the call: "Masha! Mashenka!"

"Granny!" Masha whirled round, staring up at the windows. And there, not where they had been looking but further along, was her grandmother peering out.

"Granny!" She ran back, waving excitedly.

"Shh," hissed Babka Praskovia, laying her finger on her lips. "Quiet, little one."

Granny had lost her headscarf, and without it her head looked tiny, and her gossamer white hair so thin and light it might blow away any minute. But her dark eyes twinkled as brightly as ever as she smiled down at Masha. "I'm so glad to see you, my dear."

"We came to visit you, but they wouldn't let us in." Masha was nearly crying with relief.

"Oh, the staff here, what fools!" said Babka Praskovia. "Still wet behind the ears! People were coming from all around to ask my advice before they were even born, and now they think they can boss me about. So when are you going to get me out of here, my sweetheart? I tell you, your old granny can't stand it much longer."

"They won't let us," cried Masha. "They won't tell us what's wrong with you."

"They wouldn't know what was wrong with me if it jumped up and poked them in the eye," said Granny. "It's just a bit of witchcraft, that's all. And how's our trolleybus, Masha? Is it behaving itself?"

"It came back. But I'm not living there now; I'm staying with Gena. Granny, I want to tell you all about what happened that night."

"And so you shall. But you have to take me away from here first."

"I don't know how," said Masha despairingly. "They told us to come back next Friday."

"I can't wait till then. I—" Babka Praskovia broke off. She put her finger to her lips again. "Hurry, little one, come back soon," she whispered. "Bless you!"

She disappeared from the window. Masha heard an angry shout from inside the room. "Praskovia Matveyivna! What are you doing out of bed? Get back at once."

"Don't tell me what to do, young man," Granny's thin, reedy voice replied. "And get that thing away from me. Call yourself a doctor? Don't you go sticking that into me, as if I was a pincushion."

A white-clad arm, brandishing a big hypodermic needle, appeared at the window and shut it with a bang.

"Gena! Masha!" They heard Ira calling. "Your ice creams are melting. Where are you?"

Chapter 9

Masha awoke and lay listening. But of course, she was behind concrete walls now, not in the trolleybus; here there was no guessing the weather. After a week she had got quite used to living in the hot stuffy flat again, but it still surprised her when she woke in the early mornings, her mind tangled with dreams.

She opened her eyes. The sun was lying in wonderfully clear stripes across the bed. Her head felt as though it were full of the same clear, warm light. Why was she so happy?

It was because of her dream. She'd dreamt she had been walking through the bright soft grass by the river, with her friend the Cossack girl beside her and the goat kid trotting behind. Everything shone as if polished. They had talked about the impossible place between the church and the dovecote, and Masha's two birthdays on the old and the new calendar, and it had all become clear. In the gap between the calendars was a magic time between midsummer and midsummer.

And this magic time was just like the enchanted place between the church dome and the dovecote, where treasure was buried. Impossible, but there. It was as if time and place were pieces of paper with pictures on each side. If you folded them carefully you could see both pictures at the same time, and together they combined to make a new picture, an answer to Masha's questions – when would she get her birthday present? And what was her heart's desire? Somehow it had made sense. Perfect sense.

But now as she tried to remember, the ideas slipped away and it all got confused again. Calendars and birthdays were interesting, but there were so many other things to think about: the trolleybus, and Nechipor, and the smoke on the other side of the river, and Granny. How was she going to get Granny out of hospital? It was obvious after their visit last week that she couldn't ask Ira for help. Oh, how complicated everything was!

The day got worse. When she came back from checking on the goats and the trolleybus, the big black Mercedes was parked outside the tower block, purring to itself. Masha hurried past, wondering who was watching from behind the tinted windows.

Inside the flat, Ira was flustered and Gena envious.

"The driver's been waiting for you for ages," said Ira. "Hurry up and get changed. You're to go round to Uncle Igor's for the day."

Masha's heart sank. Uncle Igor lived on an estate of brand new houses for rich people which everyone nicknamed Tsarskoe Selo, or Tsar's Village, after the place where the Russian royal family had lived before they were all killed in the revolution. Masha had been invited round several times after her mother had left, to play with Igor's daughter Anastasia.

"Do I have to go?" she asked.

"Of course you do. He is supposed to be looking after you, after all. Now, how about putting on that nice frock he gave you for your birthday."

"I don't want to wear it." Masha looked at the frilly dress with loathing. She hated wearing dresses, but to appease Ira she changed into an old one that her mother had made for her. It was very short and tight, but it was better than wearing Anastasia's cast-offs.

"Be a good girl and behave yourself," Ira said at the door. "The driver will bring you back this afternoon."

"You'll get to ride in that car again," added Gena. "That's so cool. Have a good time."

Masha didn't expect to have a good time at all. She sat gloomily in the back of the Mercedes, staring at the dashboard crowded with little gilt-framed religious icons. A furry hare's paw hung from the mirror, along with a jumble of crosses and prayer beads and a bunch of white heather. All these were for good luck. Masha knew from experience that Igor was ludicrously superstitious. Once she had been at his house when another visitor had arrived and handed him a bunch of flowers over the threshold. Uncle Igor had been angry and nervous the whole day after that because it was bad luck. Another time, his wife, Anya, had gone out and then returned five minutes later because she had forgotten something. Masha had heard Uncle Igor shouting at her for bringing bad luck on the house.

This had given Masha a wicked idea. Now when she was at Uncle Igor's she always tried to do something that was supposed to be bad luck for the head of the household. Igor had never caught her but she hoped it made him miserable, just as he had made her miserable by sending her mother away. He had promised that Mama would come back from Turkey after six months but, two years later, she still had not returned. He had promised to build them a house but, although he was the richest person Masha had ever met, he had left her and Granny to live in the trolley-bus. Her mother had said that while she was gone Uncle Igor would look after Masha, but he had never done anything. Masha was sure that the occasional presents and visits were only because his wife remembered.

His wife, Aunt Anya, was as nice as Uncle Igor was horrible. She always wore expensive-looking clothes, and had a different hairstyle every time Masha saw her. Masha thought she was very beautiful, but she also thought that, despite all her lovely clothes and make-up and her huge, fabulous house, Anya never looked happy.

Aunt Anya was waiting as the car swept through the gates and halted smoothly in the driveway. The gates swung to at once, shutting the house and garden in a thick, expensive silence.

"Hello, darling." Anya greeted her with a swift, perfumed kiss.

"Hello." There was something a little too eager about Anya's kisses and cuddles. They made Masha feel cosy and at the same time uncomfortable.

Aunt Anya's hair was a shining honey colour today, and her lips and nails were painted pale pink. She took Masha to the immaculate kitchen, where sweets and crisps, a shop-bought cake and a loaf of bread were laid out. As Aunt Anya looked into the fridge, Masha surreptitiously turned the loaf upside down. That was supposed to be bad luck.

"I haven't had a chance to say happy birthday to you yet," said Aunt Anya. "Did you get lots of nice presents?"

"Yes, I did," Masha lied. Aunt Anya's soft voice and pretty, sad smile made her very easy to talk to, and for a moment Masha wanted to tell her how disappointed she'd been that her mother hadn't sent anything for her birthday. But after all, she'd got a present from Anya instead. "Thank you very much for the book of animals," she said.

"Did you like it?"

"A lot. I brought it with me, to show you which are my favourites."

Masha took out the book, and they looked at it together on the kitchen table. Aunt Anya liked the penguins. "Let's go to the zoo sometime and see if they have any there," she suggested.

"All right," Masha agreed. "But I like the Siberian tigers best. I bet there aren't any of those in the zoo. They only live in the Far East, and Kamchatka. They're *huge*."

She turned to the page, and there was the tiger, burning orange and black against the brilliant forest green.

"I'm not sure there really are tigers in Kamchatka," Anya said. But she added hastily, "They are fantastic! Scary."

"Everything's bigger in Kamchatka," Masha said. "My papa grew up there, and he told me about it. I want to go there one day." She suddenly started feeling peculiar and sad, the old ache. Her papa had never come back from his last expedition to Kamchatka. She sometimes imagined him there, watching the tigers as he sailed on dandelion seeds as big as parachutes. At the same time, she thought he was probably dead. Only that was much harder to imagine than dandelion seeds as big as parachutes.

Aunt Anya kissed her quickly. "What an adventurous girl you are. How are you going to get to Kamchatka? Perhaps you could ride across Siberia on an elk. Are there any elks in this book?"

"What are you two looking at?" said a voice behind them.

Without them hearing, Uncle Igor had come into the room. He looked over their shoulders at the tiger.

"Ugh! What a disgusting animal," he said with a violent shudder. "I hope to God I never meet one of those. Put that picture away," he went on irritably. "Even if such revolting creatures have to exist, I don't see why I should have to look at them in my own kitchen."

Masha closed the book and put it back in her bag. Into her mind, unbidden, popped a sudden, incredible picture of a Siberian tiger in Uncle Igor's kitchen. Its enormous fat tail sweeping the cups and plates onto the floor, its vast mouth opening in a roar.

"Well, Masha, how are you?" asked Uncle Igor.

"Fine, thank you," she answered awkwardly.

"And how's the grandmother? Comfortable in the hospital, I'm sure. You know she's better off there; she's far too old to be living alone with a little girl. Perhaps you should come here and live with us, hey?" He bestowed on her his wolfish smile. "How would you like that, while we wait for your mama to come home?"

Masha found herself looking at Aunt Anya's face, sad and yearning under the careful make-up. It made her feel confused. "I like living with Granny," she said quickly. "She's coming out of hospital soon."

"We'll see," said Uncle Igor ominously. He tapped his fingers on his waistcoat, a big, dark, shiny man, like his Mercedes, and then sat down at the table and pulled a packet of cigars from his pocket. He took one out and held it under his nose, sniffing it ostentatiously.

"Mmm, delicious. What a smell." He held it out to Masha. "How about a smoke? Here, take it. Put hairs on your chest. Go on."

Masha felt angry and silly, all at once. What was she supposed to do with a cigar? She reached out hesitantly and Uncle Igor roared with laughter.

"You bad girl," he said, slapping her fingers so they stung. "Smoking already. You see, that old woman isn't bringing you up properly. I really think you ought to come here and live with us."

Masha felt herself turning pink. "I don't smoke," she said, her voice trembling. "And Mama will be back soon, so I'll live with her."

Uncle Igor leant forward. "Now, that's what I'd like to talk to you about. Have you heard from your mother lately?"

Masha felt scared by his intent stare. "Well, she sent me a postcard," she said, although she didn't want to tell Uncle Igor this at all.

"When?"

"Igor!" Aunt Anya said.

Uncle Igor ignored her. "When, and what did it say?"

"I can't remember." Tears were coming into Masha's eyes. "It was a long time ago. It had a picture of a big church on it."

"Oh, that one." Uncle Igor sat back and took out a gold lighter. He lit the cigar and drew on it with a series of puffs, blowing out a big cloud of smoke. "And since then, nothing? No letters? Maybe you've seen her."

"No. I haven't."

"Are you sure? You know, I worry about your mother and about you, little girl. I hope your granny hasn't been teaching you to tell lies."

"Igor!" said Aunt Anya again.

"No, she hasn't." Masha swallowed hard. "She's been bringing me up very well."

"All right then," said Uncle Igor. "Run along and play with Anastasia. You must tell me, though, if you do see or hear from your mother. I don't know what will happen to both of you if you don't."

"What might happen?" asked Masha bravely.

"I really don't know," he replied, tapping out the cigar ash. "Playtime. Off you go. Nastya's in the garden."

Masha ran out of the door. She felt so stupid and so angry that if she opened her mouth she thought a roar would come out, a huge, furious tiger's roar. Her face was burning hot and dried up her tears. She would have liked to have thrown all the cups and plates in there, the bread and the sweets and everything, onto the floor, crashing and smashing with each sweep of her tail, each blow of her paws.

But instead she had to go and play with Anastasia.

There she was, outside her Wendy house, waving and shouting. Masha went down the path as slowly as she possibly could.

Anastasia was eleven. She was very pretty, with long curly hair, and she always wore fancy dresses with frills of ribbon and lace. She never tired of telling Masha that she was named after a princess (despite Masha's response after a Russian history lesson, which was "Yeah, a princess who got *shot*"), and her favourite game was fairy-tale dressing up. Guess who always played the princess. Masha got to be the servant or the wicked witch, or occasionally the prince, although that was the worst role of all. At least when she was the witch she got to do nasty things to Anastasia.

She had lots of gorgeous toys, like a sandpit and a paddling pool, the Wendy house, dolls and boxes of Lego and lovely drawing things, but she was really mean with all of them.

Masha sat down in the corner of the little house with the Lego box. Anastasia was dressing one of her dolls unseasonably in what looked like a real fur coat and hat, but she soon put it aside and demanded, "What are you making?"

"A pirates' hideout." Masha rummaged for palm leaves.

They built together for a while, until Masha started adding in pieces of spaceship.

"That's wrong," Anastasia objected. "You can't use those bits."

"Why not? They're space pirates."

"No, they're not. Why've they got palm trees and parrots if they're space pirates?"

"It's a tropical planet in the Centauri galaxy," Masha invented quickly. "And they flew the parrot out all the way from earth. You can buy them on this planet for two million blips, which is Centauri money."

"That's stupid." Anastasia started taking out the spaceship pieces.

"I was building it first," said Masha crossly.

"It's my Lego," Anastasia retorted. "And they're in the Caribbean and they've never heard of your stupid Centauri galaxy."

"It's not stupid."

"Yes, it is." Anastasia crumbled up the whole construction and started throwing the bits back in the box. "I don't want to play with Lego anyway."

"Well, I don't want to play with you," said Masha. She got up and stormed out of the little house.

She hung around miserably on the smooth striped English lawn for a little while. It was always so quiet at Tsarskoe Selo, as if all the money somehow managed to exclude the cars and radios and barking dogs and shouting people all over the rest of Kiev. Finally she wandered back towards the real house. She was thirsty. Maybe Aunt Anya would give her a drink.

The kitchen door was ajar; as she came up to it she heard voices inside and paused. And then she caught her name spoken.

"Masha's only ten; you've no right threatening a little girl," she heard. That was Aunt Anya.

"For the last time, I wasn't threatening her," Uncle Igor replied.

"Oh, so what's really going on? Where exactly *is* Masha's mother?"

"Why are you asking?" Uncle Igor sounded angry. "You should know better than to ask. I don't hear you complaining about the money I make to buy you new outfits—"

"I let you carry on with your own business. All right. But don't drag a little girl into it. You bring her here to play with Anastasia, and all the time, you've got her mother mixed up in your dirty business. It's shameful! And as for the money, you know it can't buy us happiness—"

There was a sudden cracking noise, and Aunt Anya gave a squeak and fell silent. A chair scraped back.

"Why's that damned bread upside down?" shouted Uncle Igor. "Don't you know that's bad luck?" His footsteps clicked across the kitchen and the door to the hall slammed.

There was silence.

Masha stood frozen outside, hardly daring to breathe. It had sounded like Uncle Igor had hit Aunt Anya. But grown-ups didn't do things like that. And why – because the bread was upside down? Masha felt horribly guilty. What should she do? Go in and see if Aunt Anya was all right? Apologize? She couldn't hear anything inside. Finally she stuck her head cautiously round the door.

Aunt Anya was sitting very quietly at the table. She looked all right, except that she was holding one hand up to the side of her face.

Masha sidled inside, and Aunt Anya gave her a little smile. "Are you hungry or thirsty? Have a look in the fridge; you know you can help yourself to anything you want." She got up and went slowly out of the kitchen.

Masha automatically went to the fridge and opened

it. It was full of brightly coloured little cartons and packets of nice food and drink, all the kinds of things she never usually got to eat. But she didn't feel the slightest bit hungry.

At that moment, Anastasia came in from the garden. "Where's Mama?"

Masha pointed towards the hall. "I think your father hit her," she said, perhaps unnecessarily, perhaps nastily, because Anastasia went bright red and shot her a look of pure hatred before she ran out after her mother.

For the first time, Masha didn't just think about how mean Anastasia was. She thought how awful it must be having parents like Igor and Anya, and maybe that was why Anastasia wasn't very nice.

Masha guessed she was probably in disgrace after that. Feeling small and lost, she slipped outside again and round the silent house to the drive. There stood the driver, polishing the Mercedes to an even richer shine.

"It's time for me to go," Masha said. The driver turned towards her, his eyes obscured as always behind the blank sunglasses. "I can get the bus," she added quickly, disconcerted by the sight of her pale, nervous face looking back at her from the gleaming rounds of glass.

"What are you doing?"

She spun round. Igor was leaning over the pretty white balcony that looked out onto the drive, smoking and studying her in a reflective manner.

"It's time for me to go," she repeated, trying to sound bold.

"Oh, really?" He raised an eyebrow. "But we had

all sorts of nice things planned for you, young lady. All sorts of … surprises. It's a little ungrateful of you to sneak off like this. Bad manners. It's your poor upbringing showing again."

"They're waiting for me at home." Masha was angry and ashamed to hear her voice come out high and squeaky.

"And now the lies. How can they be waiting for you at home? You haven't got a home now, have you, Masha?"

"I have!" she cried. "I'm staying with Gena and Ira, and they're waiting for me, and when Granny gets better I'll live with her, and then when Mama comes back we'll live together."

"That's a lot of *and whens*. I'll add another one. *And when* your mother tells you what she was doing in Turkey, you might find you don't want to live with her after all."

"What do you mean?"

Uncle Igor simply went on smoking and gazing at her in that cold, speculative manner. At last he said, "Never mind. Come back and visit soon. You'll be living here before too long, part of one big happy family. Until then…"

He snapped his fingers at the driver.

"Take her back."

Chapter 10

Masha wandered slowly past the market towards the garages. She felt hot and sticky and unhappy. She'd been left on her own today, and she didn't know what to do with herself in an empty flat that was no longer hers. At the back of her mind she could still hear Uncle Igor saying, *You haven't got a home now, have you, Masha?*

She was lonely. She wanted to talk to someone about Granny in hospital, and about her awful visit to Tsarskoe Selo two days ago. Could Uncle Igor really make her live with him as he had threatened? And then there was her mysterious second birthday. When *was* the second midsummer's eve? Could her present be the treasure Nechipor said was buried in the enchanted place?

If only she could dream in the daytime! Then the little Cossack girl would be there and she could talk about it all, and perhaps her friend would have some answers. She put her hands on the woven belt tied round her waist and tried hard to imagine the Cossack girl: her green trousers and red boots, her smiling face under a mop of dark curly hair. But it was only a dream; she was still alone.

At the entrance to the garages, three hot dogs lay flat on their sides in the dust. One of them lifted its head and gave her a panting, doggy smile. She stepped over it carefully and went in.

"Is Fyodor Ivanovich here?" she called up to the man sitting in the watchman's cabin. He jerked his thumb over his shoulder in reply.

Behind the cabin and surrounded by garages was a small yard full of dented cars and half-finished church cupolas. The cars were brought here to have the dents smoothed out of them, and the onion-shaped domes, taller than Masha and much fatter, were here to have a skin of gleaming metal draped over their wooden skeletons. Masha watched as a man sitting on a pile of old car bumpers worked and stroked at a sheet of metal, easing it little by little to lie smooth and buttercup yellow over the curve of the dome. When it was snugly in place he looked up, and it was Fyodor Ivanovich.

"Hello," he greeted her. "Have you come to give me a hand?"

Masha looked admiringly at the half-finished cupola, with its round belly and tapering top. "It looks difficult."

"Not really. You just have to be gentle with it."

Masha sat down on a tyre near by. It was soothing watching his hands shaping the bright metal. "Where are they for?"

"The new church in Podil." Fyodor Ivanovich put

his head on one side and surveyed his work critically. "Not real gold, of course. The ones in the Lavra monastery are gold leaf."

"What about the church here, down by the river? Are you going to make any domes for that?"

"It's already got a dome. It could do with some repairs, though, you're right; it's all faded, poor thing. Maybe I can think of a way to brighten it up."

"Do you think that church can somehow … move about? I mean, be visible from particular places at particular times, and not at others?"

"That's a funny question." Fyodor Ivanovich straightened up from his makeshift seat and rubbed his back, groaning. "Some game you're playing, is it? Where's young Gena today?"

"At the dentist's, with his mother." Masha tried not to sound plaintive, but Fyodor Ivanovich's face turned compassionate. He had befriended her and Granny when they'd moved into Icarus, and he'd been unfailingly kind, helping them furnish the trolleybus, dig the outside toilet and build the goats' pen.

"Is your granny still in hospital?" he asked. "What about your mother – any word?"

Masha shook her head. Why was everybody asking about her mother, all of a sudden?

"Tell you what, Masha. I'm going to see my sister on Thursday. Why don't you come with me? The baby would love it; he took such a shine to you last time."

Fyodor Ivanovich's sister lived right across Kiev, quite close to Uncle Igor's house. The baby was actually a toddler; Masha had kept him occupied for several hours playing shops when she'd visited, putting things in and out of bags and exchanging bits of paper.

She realized Fyodor Ivanovich was trying to cheer her up. "I'd like that."

"All right. Come down here on Thursday morning and we'll go together."

"I will." Masha got up to leave. "Thanks."

Down by the river it was cooler, and the sand slipped and shuffled under her feet familiarly. She visited the goats. They chomp-chomped away at the thick grass and didn't pay her much attention.

"What shall I do?" whispered Masha into the silky pink, black-speckled ear of the kid. "Where do I find my heart's desire?"

The kid shook its head so its ears flapped, and looked meaningfully out towards the river. "Maaa," it said.

Masha looked too. A thin, grey plume of smoke rose vertically into the air above the island, like a finger pointing skywards.

"How can I get there?" Masha asked. But the kid was engrossed in a nice green willow branch.

Perhaps she would find a fisherman beside the river to take her across, so she could finally investigate the smoke. Masha was quite sure it wasn't just a shashlik party like Gena had said. It was something special, and specially to do with her. She ambled down the bank, hoping to find someone fishing beneath the willows. The faded blue dome of the church appeared on her right, and she scowled at it.

Along the riverbank a few people sunbathed, supine and almost naked in the grass. Nothing, not even a sun-dazed fish, broke the glittering water surface. The sky pulsed with light; the crickets whirred inexorably, winding the day to its pitch of brightness and heat. Masha drifted into a sort of walking dream.

A tremendous noise from the trees ahead startled her out of it. It was a snorting, roaring, whistling sound. She approached cautiously and peered through the leaves. She saw a shaded sandy hollow, almost entirely filled by the big round figure of Nechipor. The Cossack, lying comfortably with his hands folded over his bulging belly and his hat tipped over his eyes, was taking an afternoon nap. And to Masha's delight, he was leaning against a little boat. What incredible good luck!

"Nechipor!" called Masha softly. More loudly: "Hey, *Nechipor!*"

The Cossack's droopy moustache twitched once, twice, he sneezed hugely, his hat fell off and he opened his eyes.

"Who? What? Can't a fellow get even forty winks in peace? What the devil – oh, it's you," he said more calmly as he caught sight of Masha. "What d'you want, young scamp? Or do you just think it's fun to go round waking up old snoozing walruses, eh?"

"Oh no," said Masha earnestly. "I'm sorry I woke you, but I so wanted… Won't you, Nechipor – I mean, please will you take me across the river in your boat?"

"Humph." Nechipor retrieved his hat and stuck it back over his topknot. "I was planning to go fishing. Can you fish?"

"I don't know; I've never tried."

"Never tried?" he exclaimed. "Well, pickle my whiskers! All right then. Seeing as you've woken me up, you can come along and help me catch a big fat fish for my supper."

"What's so interesting about the island?" the Cossack enquired as he rowed slowly out into the river. Masha sat in the bow of the boat, amid a clutter of fishing nets and hooks.

She pointed at the smoke pencilling a faint bluish line up into the sky. "I just have this feeling," she tried to explain. "It's like trying to find the magic place between the dovecote and the church. I'm sure there's something special there."

Nechipor looked over his shoulder at the smoke. "It's a witches' wood," he muttered.

"Witches?"

"Oak trees and crows. Witches' favourites. I feel a twitching of my moustache, young Masha. I'm not sure I like it."

"What does it mean if your moustache twitches?" asked Masha, trying to see if it really was.

"It means a strange smell. A suspicious smell. I might even say the stink of that filthy old devil, may he choke on his own pong."

The oak trees ahead were a dark, sullen green, and after the dazzling glitter of the water the shadows beneath them looked black. The sun was blazing down but suddenly Masha trembled all over, as if cold air were blowing straight from those terribly dense shadows. But the trickle of smoke drew her, and the feeling that she was going to find something important grew. As the prow of the boat ran ashore onto the sand she hopped out, leaving her sandals tangled among the fishing line.

The shade beneath the trees was not as dark as it had looked from the river. Sunlight lay in brilliant yellow patches between the deeper pools of shadow. When she stepped into the shade the grass was cold, lapping round her legs like water. The way between the trees looked intensely green and enticing, laced with ferns and the twinkle of little yellow and purple blooms, and the dead afternoon stillness here was broken by the tiniest rustles and shivers, as if a thousand distant voices were whispering about her passing. She walked on towards the heart of the island with a shudder of anticipation.

Soon the sunlight reaching through the trees split into dusty spokes and there was a smell of woodsmoke. Masha emerged into a sunny clearing alive with butterflies. At the same moment as she saw a thin, red-haired woman crouched over a pot on a fire, the trees around her suddenly exploded with crows that flew shrieking and clattering into the air.

The woman jumped to her feet and turned a white, scared face towards her. It took a minute for Masha to recognize her. Then through the uproar of the crows she shrieked, "Mama!" and ran across the grass into her mother's arms.

Chapter 11

Various odd things had happened to Masha's mother. She was smaller and much thinner than Masha remembered. Her long brown hair had been cut in a short bob and dyed bright red. Oddest of all was what on earth she was doing, in grubby old jeans and a T-shirt, tending a fire on an island in the middle of the river. There were so many questions, Masha didn't know where to start.

Her mother hugged her again and again as the crows wheeled and flapped and gradually settled down again somewhere further off.

"Just look at you, so tall! And such dirty feet! Oh, how I've missed you, Mashenka." She squashed Masha into another embrace.

"But, Mama, why are you here?" Masha asked as soon as she got her nose out of her mother's shoulder. "Why didn't you come back before? Are you living here?"

"Oh, Masha." Her mother seemed unable to stop

hugging and kissing her. "I wanted to come back such a long time ago." She turned her head away and waved her hand to show she couldn't say anything else. Masha realized it was better to hug than to ask questions just now.

At last her mother wiped her eyes and sat back on her heels. "How ever did you find me, you clever girl?" she asked anxiously.

"Nechipor brought me. He's still by the river, catching a big fish for tea. I can call him—"

"No! Don't do that," Mama said with such terrified haste that Masha was startled. "Nechipor? What a funny old-fashioned name. Who is he? How do you know him?"

"He's a Cossack, a real one, with a topknot and everything. I met him on the night—" Masha stopped. This was going to be hard to explain. "Somewhere along by the river," she finished lamely. "I saw him dancing – it was brilliant."

"A Cossack? How did he know I was here?"

"He didn't know. *I* didn't know. Why *are* you here?"

Mama spoke over her. "Is he a good friend?"

Masha considered. "I think so. He grows melons on an allotment. He brought me home when I got lost, and he helped call an ambulance to take Granny to hospital."

"*To hospital?* What's happened to her?"

"It was the night of the storm," Masha explained. "She fell when… She's in hospital but she says there's nothing wrong with her except some witchcraft, and she wants to leave but they won't let her."

"So who's looking after you?"

"I'm staying with Gena and Ira."

"I can see I have a lot to catch up with," Mama said rather dazedly. "Is Granny really all right?"

"She said so. Why haven't you come to see me, Mama?"

Her mother took her hands and looked at her so seriously that Masha felt scared.

"Masha, it's hard for me to explain but you must listen carefully. It's a very big secret that I'm here. I so much wanted to come back to you but I couldn't and I still can't." She gave Masha's hands a tight squeeze. "I'm so sorry, but you must carry on living with Gena and Ira a little longer, and you must tell no one, absolutely *no one*, that I'm here. Not even Gena. Not even Granny."

"Why not?" Masha couldn't believe what she was hearing. It sounded like something out of an adventure story. "Is someone chasing you?"

After a pause, her mother sighed. "Yes."

Masha stared. "Who? Someone from Turkey? Why are they after you?"

"Mashenka, I can't tell you any more."

Masha felt suddenly angry. "Why not?"

"Maybe later."

"Later?" That sounded familiar. Tell you later, tell you when you're older, that's what grown-ups always said. "Why won't you tell me now? You thought I was old enough for you to go away to Turkey and leave me all on my own!" she shouted. "That's not fair!" She started crying, and her mother, sniffing herself, enfolded her in another huge hug.

"I can't tell anyone," she said. "Not even the police. All I can tell you is that I've run away from

— 83 —

Turkey, but very bad people in Ukraine are looking for me."

A dreadful certainty possessed Masha's mind. "Is Uncle Igor one of them?"

Masha's mother put her hand over her mouth. "Yes, he is," she said at last. "Has he asked you where I am?"

Masha nodded. "I won't tell him anything, though. Not a thing. He's horrible. He wants me to go and live with him, Mama," she added. "But now you're home I won't have to, will I?"

"He wants…" Her mother looked stunned. "He can't do that. He can't take you away from me."

"Of course he can't." Masha felt quite sanguine about Uncle Igor now that her mother was here, even if she was behaving so oddly.

"Does he want to use you against me?" Mama whispered. "Of course! He thinks if he's got you then I can never tell the truth about what happened…"

"Mama?" Masha shook her knee. "Mama! What are you talking about?"

Her mother seemed to come out of a horrified daze. "Nothing. I've been on my own for so long, Masha, I've got into a silly habit of talking to myself. Don't laugh at me."

"I won't." Masha patted Mama's shoulder consolingly, although it felt strange to be doing so, as if her mother was just a little girl too. "Mama, why did you let Uncle Igor send you to Turkey?"

"Because I was very silly and very … very hopeful," said her mother sadly. "And now I'm in awful trouble."

"Have you done something that's not allowed?

Against the law, I mean?" To Masha's shock, her mother stared at her for a long moment: a lost, blank, unseeing stare. "You have?"

"Sort of. No, nothing. At least..." Her mother floundered. "No, Masha, I've done nothing wicked. But there are people in Turkey, and here, like Igor, who are doing things against the law, and they're the ones who are chasing me now."

Masha remembered the Cossack in his allotment, clapping his hand to his knife when she mentioned where her mother was. "Nechipor says Ukrainian girls and women are made slaves in Turkey," she said. At the time, she'd thought he was being ridiculous. "He said his heart was burning to take revenge for it. You weren't ... you weren't actually made a slave, were you?"

Her mother looked startled. "I suppose ... sort of. But revenge isn't so easy when it's your own country-men. When it's someone you thought was your friend..."

Masha felt as if the whole conversation was sliding out of control, into some dark, unreal dream. She held her mother's shoulder tightly, making sure she was solid, she was really there. "So you're hiding now? How did you get here anyway? It's an island."

"I know. It was the strangest thing," said her mother. "In fact, you'll probably think I've gone a bit mad. I walked here."

"You can't have!"

"But I did." Mama leant forward to poke at the cooking pot again. The mossy, freshwater smell of boiling fish rose out of it. "It was the night of the storm. Do you remember?"

Masha shivered excitedly. "Of course I remember."

Mama settled herself back more comfortably on the ground, Masha in her lap.

"I'd just arrived in Kiev that day, at the end of a long, terrible journey all the way from Turkey. I was so tired! I walked right across the city to get here, as the sky got darker and darker, and I'd just reached the sand by the river when – *crash! bang!* – the storm started."

"Go on."

"I hadn't decided what to do. I so much wanted to see you, my sweetheart." A tight squeeze. "But the rain was pouring down, the thunder was crashing and the lightning flashing, and I got completely lost. I walked and walked and walked through the trees and allotments, and then I really think I must have been dreaming, because I thought I saw a trolleybus driving along."

"And then what?"

"I started running after it. I was soaked and frozen and I just wanted some shelter. But it disappeared, and soon the storm eased off. I found a sheltered patch under some trees and I sat down, and I must have fallen asleep. When I woke it was already sunny, so I got up and walked around to find out where I was – and here I was, on the island!"

"And what about the trolleybus?"

Her mother laughed. "I think I must have been seeing things, don't you?"

"I *know* you weren't seeing things," said Masha importantly. "Now I'm going to tell you what happened to *me* on the night of the storm."

How on earth am I not going to tell anyone? Masha wondered as she walked back to Gena's house. She felt so puzzled and excited and above all happy that her mother had come back, it was going to be very hard not to talk about it. But her mother had warned her again and again that she must keep quiet, so she hadn't even told Nechipor as he rowed her back, although she was longing to ask what he'd meant when he'd talked about slaves and Turkey. Most of all, Masha wanted to stay on the island with Mama, to share the soup she was making from fish caught with an old hook and line she'd found. But her mother said she had to go back, otherwise people would become suspicious.

"You've got to pretend nothing has happened," she said. "I'm so sorry, but you do understand it's important, don't you?"

Masha nodded. Even if she didn't know exactly why people were chasing her mother, if Uncle Igor was involved she was sure it was serious. Many of the rich people in Ukraine, with big new houses and Mercedes cars, belonged to the mafia and had made their money from sinister and illegal business. This was common knowledge, but it had never seemed quite real to Masha before. Now she realized her mother had somehow got involved in Uncle Igor's business, and she understood more of Aunt Anya's words that she had overheard in the kitchen at Tsarskoe Selo.

I won't tell Uncle Igor anything, however much he asks, she promised herself determinedly as she climbed the stairs to the flat. Nothing at all.

But there was very bad news waiting for her when she arrived.

"Your Uncle Igor called," Ira told her. Masha

suddenly felt cold all over. "He wants you to go and live with him until your granny comes out of hospital."

"Oh no!" cried Masha. "Why? I don't want to. Why can't I stay here with you?"

"Of course you could stay here with us," said Ira. "But he was really rather insistent. Why don't you want to go? I'm sure they'd look after you very well."

"But Mama said—" Masha stopped abruptly, realizing she'd almost let out the secret already. "I know Mama wouldn't want me to go," she said. "He's horrible, he's really horrible!"

"Masha, that's a naughty thing to say," Ira scolded in her schoolteacher voice. "Of course he's not horrible. Anyway, he definitely wants you to live with him and I don't think I can say no."

"Why not?" Masha wailed. "Please don't make me go!"

Ira looked troubled, and it suddenly occurred to Masha that she seemed afraid of Igor, just as her mother was. "Because... Because he's supposed to be looking after you," she said finally. "Really, Masha, you're being silly. I'm sure you'll be fine there, and you can come and play with Gena whenever you like. Anyway, it's only as long as your grandmother's in hospital."

"You mean, if Granny comes back I won't have to go?" asked Masha eagerly.

"I suppose so."

Masha cornered Gena in his room, where he was lying on the bed reading comics.

"Gena," she whispered urgently. "I need your help. We've got to think of a plan to get Granny out of hospital."

Chapter 12

Outside the hospital ward the same nurse sat at her desk, reading a book and drinking tea. She looked up when she heard Gena and Masha approaching.

"Not you two again," she said disapprovingly.

"Can we see my grandmother, please?"

"No." The nurse returned to her book. It had a picture of a red-haired woman on the cover, her enormous bosom popping out of her dress, in the arms of a man with no shirt on.

"Didn't I tell you to come back on Friday?" the nurse said at last, when they didn't move. "The doctor's busy and your grandmother's to see no one."

"We've brought her some more things," said Masha. "To cheer her up. But we had to leave the bag at the front desk. The man there said it was too big, and we should come up here and tell someone to fetch it."

"Oh, for goodness' sake. What are you expecting me to do about it? Your grandmother will just have to wait, or do without."

"Please, can't you come and collect it?" said Gena. "We'll have to take it home again otherwise, and it's got such nice things in it. Smoked fish, even some caviar."

"Black caviar," Masha added persuasively. "The best."

The nurse heaved an exasperated sigh, but it did not hide the greed that sparked in her eyes. She closed the book and lumbered out of her chair. "Oh, all right then." She waved the two children in front of her. "What are you standing there for?"

"We thought we'd wait here for you," said Masha.

"Then think again. If it's such a big parcel, you can certainly help me carry it. It's not my job to lug things like that around." She gave Masha a push down the corridor and marched behind them both like a guard.

The hospital entrance hall was deserted and stifling in the noonday heat. There appeared to be no one behind the high reception desk, but when the nurse peered over it, she fell back with a gasp of surprise.

"Who on earth are you?" she demanded.

The round bulk of Nechipor, resplendent in his embroidered shirt, his face pink and shiny, emerged enormously from behind the desk.

"I'd almost given you up for lost," he bellowed. "Why, if you knew what was waiting for you you'd come running, not minching down here like a cow with worms."

The nurse bristled, but before she could speak another head bobbed up beside Nechipor. This head was covered in wispy brown hair and wore a wondering expression in its bleary eyes. It was the hospital doorman.

"Amazing," said the head thickly. "Amazing what they still make in the village." It disappeared again with a slight hiccup.

The nurse leant over the desk and brought it back into view by heaving on the doorman's collar.

"Sergey Sergeyich, what is going on here?" she snapped.

"Lucky grandmother on your ward," Sergey Sergeyich said, with a dreamy smile. "They've brought her such wonderful things. Expect you'll get to have some too. Lucky."

Nechipor knocked on a door in the wall behind the desk. "All the best from the village," he boomed. "Poppy seed cakes, tender hams, sausages, the best *salo* you ever tasted."

"They said there was caviar," the nurse said stolidly.

"There might be caviar," Nechipor agreed airily. "I'm not saying there isn't. There are even better things than caviar."

"Better…" echoed the doorman, blinking and swaying.

The nurse looked at them both suspiciously. "So where is all this stuff you've brought? I suppose I can take it up to the old woman, although it's a lot of trouble for me."

Nechipor knocked on the door again. "Sergey Sergeyich told me to put it in here, out of the way." He opened the door and stuck his head inside. "Yes, still here. Hasn't run off anywhere, although I'll tell you, there's a roast duck that's so fresh and tender I'm surprised it hasn't flown away. Please come and take it, madam. I'm worried that if I carry it myself I won't be able to resist the smell and I'll have to start eating."

The nurse came round the desk and put her head through the doorway. Nechipor gave her a smart push inside, closed the door and turned the key in the lock.

"Off we go!" he boomed, swinging a big sack out from under the desk. "Won't you come too, Sergey Sergeyich? I'm sure the grandmother will invite you to partake of something."

A muffled banging came from behind the door.

Sergey Sergeyich upended a little glass tumbler so it stood on his nose. "Where's the nurse gone? She was right here. Nurse?" He shook his head vaguely. "Strange banging noise…"

Masha started to kick one heel loudly against the wall. "It's me," she said quickly. "I'm bored waiting here; I want to take all these presents to Granny. Let's go."

Gena drummed on the desktop. "Me too. So bored. Come on."

Nechipor heaved the sack over his shoulder and picked up a nearly empty bottle and a second glass. He handed the bottle to the doorman.

"Sergey Sergeyich," he said. "Another toast awaits when we give Granny her presents. Lead the way."

Sergey Sergeyich's face brightened. He took the bottle and set off waveringly up the hallway.

The hospital corridors were quiet and empty; Masha supposed everyone was having lunch. But Sergey Sergeyich and Nechipor didn't seem to want to keep quiet. "There is another bottle, isn't there?" the doorman kept asking, and, "The grandmother will invite me to drink something, won't she?"

"Bottles and bottles and bottles," carolled Nechipor. His face was even rosier and shinier than usual and his moustache had a ferocious curl. "Nectar!" he shouted with a kind of reverent exuberance, slapping the doorman on the back. "Drink of the gods!"

"Shh!" said Masha nervously, but there was no hushing the Cossack, who strode along with the sack over his shoulder, singing. Several disapproving heads looked out of the wards as they passed, but whether intimidated by the sight of the huge Cossack or reassured to see Sergey Sergeyich, none of them said anything.

When they reached Granny's ward at the top of the stairs, the door was locked.

"Oh no!" Masha cried. "The nurse must have the key. What shall we do?"

"Call that a lock?" snorted Nechipor. He picked up the spoon from the nurse's abandoned teacup and jiggled it around in the keyhole. The door opened.

"What have we here?" Nechipor roared, swaggering into the ward. "Good afternoon, ladies."

The room was full of grandmothers. Most of them were lying in narrow, sagging iron beds, the thin sheets pulled up to their chins. Two were sitting up playing chess on the mattress with pieces made ingeniously out of cigarette packets, and one was knitting a long brown stocking. At the end of the room, another was smoking furtively by the window.

"Who have you come to visit, dear?" the knitting old woman said eagerly to Masha.

"My granny." Masha looked in vain around the long room. "I can't see her."

"Take your pick," said the one by the window. "Lots of grannies here."

Masha walked uncertainly down the ward, past all the faded blue eyes watching her hungrily. Only the two chess players never looked up.

"Granddaughter!" cried one old woman in a grubby cotton wrap. "Come here, my love." But it wasn't Masha's grandmother and she hurried past.

Granny was lying in a bed near the end. Her feet made a little bump at the bottom of the sheet, and her snowy white hair made a ruffle at the top. She was lying quite still with her eyes closed.

"Granny," said Masha uncertainly. "Granny, it's me."

Granny's eyes popped open, dark and twinkling. "Mashenka, there you are," she said. "What took you so long?"

"I came as soon as I could." Masha gave her a hug. How small and frail she felt! But Granny gave her a strong, hard kiss on her forehead.

"Better late than never," she said. "Come to get me out, have you?"

"Of course. We brought Nechipor to save you."

The Cossack advanced down the ward, and Granny regarded him without surprise. "Hello," she greeted him. "Thank you for your help."

"Lord save us, I'm happy to be of service," said Nechipor. "Excuse my asking, Babka Praskovia. Can you walk, or shall I carry you?"

"It's my leg. Getting better, but I can't be quick." Granny sat up and patted her hair. "Don't suppose you brought my headscarf, did you, child? They took it away, the greedy grabbing creatures. Took everything. Would have had my soul if they could." She felt around under the bed for her slippers – old hospital slippers, not the pair they had brought for her earlier, Masha noticed – and put on the cardigan that Masha held out.

The rest of the grandmothers watched these preparations with astonishment and envy. In the next bed, a little, pale old lady beckoned to Gena.

"Where's she going?" she quavered in a tiny voice.

"Home, of course," Gena answered.

"Home…" Tears came into her dim blue eyes. "Won't you take me home too?"

"But I don't know where your home is," said Gena uncomfortably.

"Don't take any notice," interrupted the woman by the window. "Don't listen, or they'll all want to go with you, and you'll have fifty grannies to deal with instead of one. Why, I might even come with you myself." She had smoked her cigarette right down to the end, and now she threw it outside regretfully.

"Granddaughter!" That was the old woman who had called out to Masha before. "Come here, come over to me."

"Let's go." Masha took her grandmother's arm to help her up. "Quick as we can, before the nurse comes back, or the doctor."

They set off up the ward. Granny's left leg was stiff and she could only walk very slowly, leaning on Masha.

Sergey Sergeyich was standing in front of the door, holding the empty bottle and glass accusingly. "Where's the drink? Celebration drink. You promised."

"So we did." To Masha's dismay, Nechipor swung the bag down from his shoulder.

"We should run while no one's here," said Masha anxiously.

"Always time for a drink," was all Nechipor said, sticking his head inside the sack. "Isn't that right, Sergey Sergeyich?"

"Exactly," the doorman concurred with greedy emphasis.

Nechipor emerged brandishing a bottle of pale golden liquid, from which he poured a generous measure for the doorman and another for himself. "Real Cossack *samogon*. Your health, Sergey Sergeyich."

The two men downed their glassfuls with much gasping and smacking of lips.

"Hits the spot," said Sergey Sergeyich, his eyes watering. "Just one more, eh?"

"Oh, let's go," pleaded Masha. But there was no budging the Cossack.

"No hurry, no hurry," he said, pouring out more drink. "Fire in the stomach, iron in the soul, that's what this is." He raised his glass. "The second toast," he announced, "is for the ladies. Ladies, we salute you! Your beauty, your charms! May your fingers be always nimble, your cooking pots full and your husbands faithful!"

Down the ward, the rows of old women gazed at him with sad vacancy. Granny gave a loud snort.

"May your husbands never be drinkers, if you're cursed with them at all," commented the woman by the window. "Give us a fag, and stop blethering your nonsense."

"*Now* let's go," Masha urged as Nechipor tossed back the glassful.

At that moment, the door flew open.

"There they are!" shrieked the nurse. With her was a doctor, a beefy orderly and two security guards in combat fatigues who advanced purposefully, rolling up their sleeves.

"Hooligans! Terrorists! That's the thug who locked me up," shouted the dishevelled nurse, pointing at Nechipor.

"I'll call the police," the doctor said, "as soon as we get our troublesome old woman back in bed where she belongs."

"I don't belong there and never did, and you're nothing but a jailer," Granny retorted.

"We're taking her home; that's where she belongs," Masha said defiantly. But the nurse grabbed her ear and began to pull her away from Granny. It was so painful that Masha screamed.

"What's all this? Over my dead body!" roared Nechipor as the guards closed in. He gave the sack on the ground a kick, and a small, hard, round green object rolled out.

There was a sudden silence. The grandmothers stared from their beds. The guards stopped dead in their tracks and Masha saw their eyes go wide with fear.

"No, it can't be…" breathed one.

"Hand grenade!" shouted the other.

As if the shout had broken a spell, they both turned tail and ran out of the room.

Another small green ball rolled out of the sack.

"Take cover!" yelled one of the guards as he scram-bled back down the stairs. The doctor and the orderly suddenly dashed for the door and disappeared after them. The nurse, bewildered, peered closer at the objects on the floor.

"Come along, quickly!" Nechipor scooped Granny up into his arms and strode towards the door. Gena followed, grabbing the sack.

"Hand grenade?" said the nurse. Then she shouted, "Come back, you fools! Call yourself guards? Call yourself Afghan veterans? Idiots!" She tightened her grip on Masha's ear, panting, "I'll keep you here at least, you little minx."

The doorman had watched the whole affair in a daze. "What are you standing there for?" the nurse bawled at him. "Help me!"

Sergey Sergeyich obligingly took hold of Masha's arm. Nechipor was already halfway down the stairs with Granny, but Gena looked round and saw what was happening. Almost without thinking, he ran back and upended the sack he had picked up. A dozen more of the hard green ovals tumbled out and went bowling along the floor.

As they rolled around their ankles, the nurse and the doorman stumbled helplessly. Sergey Sergeyich sat down with a bump. "Never drink again," Masha heard him say plaintively as she pulled free and ran after the others. The nurse tried to follow but her feet were hopelessly tangled up in the rolling objects. She was left behind as Gena and Masha tore down the corridors and out into the sunshine, following Nechipor still carrying Granny like a child in his arms.

Chapter 13

They were out of the gates and trying to hail a taxi when they realized they were not alone. Nechipor had set Granny down and was attempting to dust her off. There at his elbow Masha and Gena suddenly noticed the old woman who had been smoking by the window in the ward.

Granny regarded her with disfavour. "Oh, you're here, are you, you baggage," she greeted her.

"No need to be rude," replied the old woman, amiably enough. "We're on different sides, but all the same I'm grateful to you for getting me out of there." She bent down and fished under the hedge that surrounded the hospital grounds, pulling out a little old wooden cart on pram wheels. "Stole my bottles, curse 'em," she muttered, looking inside. "Well, I'll be off. Might do you a good turn one day, you never know. Owe you one." She grinned at Gena and Masha and pinched Nechipor's bottom.

Just then a taxi drew to a stop, and in the flurry of

climbing in they didn't see where she went.

"Who was she and why don't you like her?" asked Masha as they drove away.

"Old witch," Granny replied, preoccupied with trying to tie Nechipor's handkerchief over her head.

"But you're a witch!" Gena burst out in astonishment before he could help himself.

Masha glared at him. But Granny only replied, "Well, like she said then, we're on different sides. The impudent besom, hitching a ride on our escape." She sniffed disgustedly, then leant back and closed her eyes. "Well, it's a breath of fresh air to be out of there. I feel better already. Now, take me home."

Masha had another question. "Nechipor, what *were* those green things inside the sack? They weren't really hand grenades, were they?"

Nechipor chuckled rosily. "Came in pretty useful, didn't they? It's not quite what I was growing them for, but bless my bonnet, didn't those guards run, the lily-livered, kitten-hearted—"

"*Growing* them?"

Gena burst out laughing. "They were melons! Little unripe watermelons! Those guards are going to feel so stupid when they realize."

"Melons!" Masha began to laugh too. But then she said, "Those were the melons you were taking such care of, Nechipor. Now you won't have any."

"Plenty more where they came from," said the Cossack cheerfully. "Anyway, I wouldn't have missed today for anything. Haven't had so much fun in years."

It was an uncomfortable ride. Nechipor fell asleep in the front seat and snored enormously, filling the car with *samogon* fumes. Neither Masha nor Gena had any money, so they had to go to the flat and persuade the taxi driver to wait while Gena ran upstairs to beg some from his mother. When he'd been paid the man drove off, grumbling, but by then Ira had come down and was clamouring to know what had happened.

Puzzlingly, Nechipor had managed to disappear completely during the kerfuffle with the taxi driver, just as he had the night of the trolleybus ride. Masha was rather relieved; it made things easier to explain. They all trooped inside, and Granny told a version of events that, without lying, stopped Ira's questions.

"They had no reason to keep me in hospital; I'm perfectly well," she said firmly. "When Masha and Gena came to see me today, I told them so. And we left. Simple as that."

With Ira's help, Granny propped her bad leg on a stool in the kitchen and folded her hands in her lap. "What are we going to do now, eh, Masha? Go back to our trolleybus?"

Masha had told Granny the whole story of the ride in the thunderstorm, whispering in her ear in the taxi, and Granny had been entirely calm about it. But Masha still felt slightly nervous of Icarus. "I suppose so," she replied doubtfully. "If we don't, Uncle Igor might still take me away."

Granny frowned. "What's Igor got to do with any-thing?"

"He did mention that, as Masha's guardian, he'd like to take Masha to live with him and his family," Ira put in, rather defensively.

"But I don't have to, now you're back; and any-way, Mama— " Masha broke off, realizing once again that she'd nearly given away the secret. She longed to tell Granny about her mother's return and the trouble she was in. But she remembered that she had to keep quiet.

"It's a good thing you got me out of that hospital," Granny said. "Igor's a nasty piece of work and I don't want you to go to him; I want you to stay with me."

"Are you really well enough to go back to the trolleybus, Babka Praskovia?" Ira asked. "It's a little isolated, after all, and your leg is so bad. You would be welcome to stay here for a bit with Masha if you like."

"That's kind of you," said Granny, "but I think we should go home."

At that moment, the phone rang. Ira went out into the hall to answer it, and they heard her voice raised in surprise or anger. When she came back, she was flushed and frowning.

"That was your Uncle Igor. Somehow he knows that you've left the hospital, Babka Praskovia. He said something about you escaping, leaving without permission, frightening the staff—"

"Oh, what nonsense," said Granny. "I had a right to leave if I wanted to, didn't I? But how ever did he find out?"

"I don't know. I suppose he must have called there for some reason." Ira sat down, puffing indignantly. "He's on his way round here now to see what's going on. I really think he's overstepping the mark a little. He said he couldn't allow me to poke my nose into his affairs any more, for goodness' sake. Who does he think he is? I'll shelter you here as long as I like!"

Masha saw that now Uncle Igor had been rude to Ira, she was so annoyed she had forgotten to be frightened of him. But the fact that he already knew about Granny's escape made Masha more frightened than ever. Perhaps the police would come, as the doctor in the hospital had threatened, and take Granny away again, or put them all in prison. Perhaps Uncle Igor would drag her away by force to his big house and lock her up. Thinking about it made tears start to her eyes. She hid her face in Granny's shoulder.

When Ira and Granny saw she was crying, they made a big fuss of her.

"Now don't you worry, Masha dear," said Ira. "Everything will be fine. You'll stay here with me, and your granny too, for as long as you like, until your mother comes home, because I expect she'll be home soon – I'm sure she will." That just made Masha cry harder than ever.

She was still snivelling when the doorbell rang.

"Now you just go into the other room with Gena," Ira said firmly. "Your granny and I will sort everything out, don't you worry."

"I won't have to live with Uncle Igor?" Masha swallowed down the sobs.

"I promise you won't have to, all right? You just sit in the other room, and you won't even have to see him." Ira shooed the two children gently along the corridor, and shut the door before going to answer the bell.

Gena looked out of the window. The Mercedes was sitting like a great sleek black beetle in front of the building. As he watched, a scruffy stray dog trotted up and sniffed at the rear wheel. Then it lifted its leg. The driver's window slid down and a burning cigarette butt flew out and hit it hard on the nose. The dog whimpered and slunk away. The window rolled silently up again.

In the room, Masha had pulled a big book off the shelf and was studying it, still occasionally wiping the tears from her cheeks.

"It'll be all right, Masha," said Gena. "We managed to get your granny out of hospital, didn't we? If we did that we can do anything."

"But what if the police come for us?"

"We didn't do anything wrong." Gena sounded more confident than he felt. "I mean, there can't be a law against throwing melons on the floor, can there? I bet those guards are too embarrassed to tell anyone what happened anyway."

Masha smiled tearily. She looked back at the book, which she'd just opened as something, anything, to take her mind off Uncle Igor there in the kitchen. It was a world atlas, and it had fallen open at the Turkey page. She read the city names. *Ankara. Istanbul.* She remembered the postcard her mother had sent her, over a year ago, had been from Istanbul, and the church had been called St Sophia, like the church in Kiev.

She turned the pages slowly. *Bulgaria. Moldova. Ukraine.* She traced the roads with her finger, wondering if Mama had come along them on her way home to Kiev. *Belarus. Russia.* She flicked through Siberia. That was where she'd like Uncle Igor to be. That bit there, where there was nothing at all marked, not a road, not a town, nothing, just a great freezing river and unending wastes of killing snow. And tigers. Siberian tigers, bigger and more terrible than anything in the whole world, to terrify him to death.

It was no good. She just couldn't forget what was going on. She shut the book and went over to the door.

"Where are you going?" asked Gena.

"Shh!" Masha opened the door very gently. She tiptoed along the corridor and into the bathroom. There was a little window in the wall, just below the ceiling, that looked out into the kitchen. Masha climbed onto the edge of the bath. If she balanced against the basin she could see and hear everything that was happening.

Uncle Igor was sitting right below the window; she could see the pink spot on top of his head where he was going bald. There was a big bunch of plastic-looking dark red roses in front of him on the table.

"I'm sorry to break the news to you," Uncle Igor was saying. "I can see it's a shock. Of course, I don't really know what happened. But it's clear your grand-daughter has somehow become involved in affairs in Turkey that are, well, illegal, to say the least. Not to mention immoral."

Masha stared down at Granny and Ira, who both sat very still. Then Granny said, "Whatever my grand-daughter may or may not have done, I don't see that it's any of your business. And how do you know about it anyway?"

"You forget, Sveta put various things into my hands before she left," Igor said softly. Sveta was Masha's mother's name. "She asked me to look after Masha, for example. As I've reminded you before. And that's what I'd like to do. I trust you'll let Masha come to me, once you've thought about all the advantages she would have. I have a large house, my income is, um, adequate. My wife adores children, and my darling Nastya would love to have a little sister to play with – they could share so many things."

Be Anastasia's little sister? Masha almost fell off the bath in horror.

"You still haven't answered my question: how do you know what happened to Sveta in Turkey?" Granny said sharply.

"I have my contacts," said Igor. "You don't have a phone, Babka Praskovia. You don't have an address. You're an old lady; you live in an abandoned trolleybus. Who would even notice if something happened to you? You know you can't help Sveta now, and you aren't fit to look after Masha. Give her over to my care."

"All in good time." Granny suddenly bent down and began rummaging in a bag under the table, muttering to herself.

"What's that? What are you saying?" Igor looked nervously under the table.

Granny sat up again and, reaching over, appeared to slip something into his jacket pocket.

"What?" Igor put his hand in the pocket. He felt around quickly and pulled his hand out again, empty. He glared at Granny. "What are you doing? What did you put in there?"

"Oh, nothing, nothing." Granny looked innocent. "Where were we? Oh yes, I'm an old woman; I live in an abandoned trolleybus. And whose idea was that, may I ask? Who moved us there with promises to build us a new home? Who lured my granddaughter away with promises of well-paid work abroad? Oh yes, I'm an old woman. And I'm wise in ways you can only imagine. Remember that. Because I remember everything. Especially grudges."

Igor stood up quickly. He felt around again in his pocket, breathing heavily.

"Well," he said in a very reasonable voice, "I won't rush you. I don't want to split up a family. I have your interests at heart; I want only what is best for dear Masha. I hope and trust you'll see that she's better off with me. Because, I'm terribly sorry to say, there is nothing but bad in her mother, and to have anything more to do with her could work out very unfortunately, for all of you. I wouldn't answer for the consequences."

Granny and Ira stared up at him silently.

"I'm afraid Sveta may come back here, tell you some ridiculous lies, try to take Masha away. Of course you'll tell me if she does. If you don't, I'll find out anyway, and so will the police. And I'd hate for you to get into trouble."

"Thank you," said Granny. "I think we understand." She looked into the bag under the table again. Igor's hand immediately went to his pocket, and Masha could see the bulge of his fingers scurrying around in it frantically.

"Well, I'll be off," he said, and the menace cut right through the reasonableness of his voice. "I'm out of town tomorrow, but I shall expect to hear from you the day after that. I know you'll take good note of my advice."

Ira made a small move to rise. "I'll see myself out," Uncle Igor said.

As soon as Masha heard the flat door close she scrambled down from the bath and ran into the kitchen.

"What did he mean, Mama is bad?" she cried. "Why did he say the police would find out? You won't let him take me away, will you, Granny? What did you put in his pocket?"

"Hush now, hush," said Granny, putting her arms round Masha.

"Were you listening?" demanded a pale, flustered Ira. "I told you to stay in the other room."

"You can't believe him," Masha insisted. "He's the bad one, not Mama. You can't let him take me to his horrible house, you just can't."

"I won't, Mashenka, I won't," Granny said. "Of course I don't believe him. I know my Sveta better than that. She may have got into trouble in Turkey, but she's no criminal."

Masha looked at Ira, and saw a strange expression of indecision and fear on her face. "Oh, but..." she said. "The police..." she tried again. "You know, maybe Sveta did get involved—" She stopped and put her head in her hands. "I just don't know what to think."

"Well, I do," said Masha loudly. "My mama only got mixed up in something wrong because Uncle Igor sent her to some awful place with bad people, and she was just stupid and didn't know. And I don't see why I should call him uncle any more, because he isn't my uncle and he's never going to take me away, so there."

"Quite right," said Granny. "Good girl. Pull yourself together, Ira. Make us a nice cup of tea, and we'll all feel better."

"What did you put in his pocket anyway?" Ira got up obediently to fill the kettle. "All of a sudden he couldn't wait to leave."

Granny's dark eyes twinkled. "Nothing." She gave

Masha a kiss. "It was you, Mashenka, who told me how superstitious Igor is. I thought I'd see if it was true. I was mumbling the recipe for borscht and in this bag…" She looked under the table and picked it up. "What is in this bag? Beetroot." She pulled one out by its cropped green leaves. "But if he wanted to think this is my bag of spells and I was putting a curse on him, well, that's his business. It'll worry him for a few hours."

And that's the second time today, thought Masha, that we've done something completely silly and harmless and made people who are stronger than us run away. The security guards from the hospital had been in a war, and she was sure now that Igor was involved in all sorts of unimaginable crimes. Maybe all Granny and Nechipor had done was to make such people expect the same bad things from others as they had done themselves.

She tugged Granny's hand. "But couldn't you put a real curse on Igor, so he'd leave us alone?" And I wouldn't have to be scared of him any more, she added to herself.

"You have to be careful with such things. All magic has two sides: it does harm and it does good. A curse has the side that goes outwards to the cursed one, and the side that comes back to the one who cursed. In time, maybe I'll do it. But it might be the end of me. Better to let him imagine it."

"But that won't last, will it?" Masha was thinking how Igor had still left with a threat.

"No," said Granny. "It won't. Oy oy oy, too many questions. My leg aches. Where's that tea?"

Gena came into the kitchen. "Did you give Igor

fleas or something? I saw him outside and he was feeling in all his pockets and scratching away. Hey, what are these flowers for?"

"Congratulations for getting out of hospital," Granny said sourly. "Congratulations indeed. For escaping from prison."

Masha leant over to sniff the fat, perfect, red–black roses Igor had brought. They smelt of petrol.

Chapter 14

Masha lay in bed looking at the faint summer light still coming in through the window. She was thirsty and knew she couldn't sleep. She could hear bursts of laughter floating up from the dim street below, the soft strumming of a guitar.

They had not gone back to the trolleybus. Granny's leg seemed to be getting worse; when she had tried to get up from her seat in the kitchen she could hardly move it. It was obvious she couldn't make the short walk down to the sandy riverbank. So Masha had been sent to bed in her old room again, and now she was lying waiting for Granny to join her.

She just had to get a drink. Quietly she got out of bed and padded into the hall in her bare feet.

Ira and Granny were still sitting in the kitchen.

"I'm sorry," Ira was saying. "Sveta was my best friend for years; Masha is almost like a daughter. But I have Gena to think of. I don't know what Sveta has been doing in Turkey; I don't want to know. I can

believe it wasn't her fault, but she'll have to keep quiet
to protect Masha; Igor's seen to that. I just can't get
mixed up in anything to do with the mafia, not with
Gena. I don't want to throw you out but you can't
stay here."

She saw Masha in the doorway. "What are you
doing, eavesdropping again?" she said angrily.

"I wasn't! I came to get a drink, that's all."

"Well, all right." Ira, rather shamefaced, poured
Masha a glass of water and ruffled her hair when she
gave it to her. "Now get back to bed, there's a good
girl. Sweet dreams."

Sweet dreams, thought Masha dismally, climbing
back into bed. What was happening? Was Ira, who'd
been so nice all this time, going to send them away?
Did she believe Igor that Mama was a criminal? No
one would tell her what Igor had said her mother had
done. Oh, these grown-ups, they wouldn't explain
what was really happening, but they weren't helping;
they weren't looking after her. It was like living in a
house that suddenly fell down, like discovering the
roof that was meant to keep off the rain was made of
cardboard. She'd waited so long for her mother to
come home and take care of her again, and now that
Mama was back she was useless and frightened and
had done something stupid just as Masha might have
done. And even Granny, her beloved Granny. It was
all right to play tricks, but that wouldn't make life go
back to normal. Why couldn't Granny do something
to really stop Igor?

Masha thought about the witchcraft Granny had
done for her, back in the village years ago, when she'd
had all those bad dreams about snakes. Pouring molten

wax into water, she knew, was a way of divining what was frightening a person and then stopping the fear. If she poured wax into water, Masha wondered, would she find out what had happened to Mama in Turkey? There was a small, fierce fire of anger burning inside her; anger that her silly mother had not told her everything and would not tell her. She had to *know* – wasn't that what this was all about? Why Igor wanted to take her away to live with him. Where Mama had really been and what she had done.

She suddenly remembered what Mama had said, when she'd started talking to herself on the island. *He thinks if he's got you then I can never tell the truth about what happened…* Even Mama had admitted that it was all about knowing. Masha didn't understand exactly why, but she was suddenly sure that if she knew the truth about her mother, Igor would no longer be able to threaten them. Knowing would make the fear and uncertainty go away. That was why her grandmother poured wax into water. That was why Igor bullied her and Granny and Ira and even his wife—

There was one other person who knew what it was all about. That was why she had argued with Igor, and he had hit her. Nice, sad Aunt Anya.

With these awful thoughts in her head, she'd never be able to sleep. Never ever again. If only she could tell all this to someone! Masha closed her eyes and curled herself up into a ball of angry unhappiness, pulling the sheet over her head.

But there were other things to talk about, after all. The river was frozen over, a great gleaming sheet stretching away to the island, and there were exploded stars and flattened bubbles like pancakes caught in the ice.

"If you think about it," Masha said to the little Cossack girl, "the air inside that bubble is already old. When the ice melts in spring it will be a tiny bit of winter that comes out."

"Baaah humbug," said the goat kid. It was standing on the ice, all four legs splayed out so that it didn't fall over. "Are you ready for your second birthday yet, Masha? Do you know your heart's desire?"

"But we still don't know when her second birthday is," said the Cossack girl, turning a graceful pirouette on one red skate.

"Silly," said the kid. "Look down there and you'll see it."

Masha lay on her tummy and pressed her nose to the glassy ice. It was like looking through the night sky, past sprinklings of rainbow-edged galaxies, stars like bursting globes of mercury. There was yellow sunlight underneath it, and yes, there was the river-bank, with willow trees and allotments, and the church with its dome, and the old wooden dovecote, but it was all inside out.

"Go on, pull it up," said the kid.

There was a hole in the thick ice, one of those round tunnels bored by an ice-fisherman. Masha put her hand into it. Down, down, until she caught hold of something. It felt like a wooden pole. She pulled, but nothing moved.

The Cossack girl put her hands round Masha's waist, and they both pulled together. Still nothing moved.

The kid took hold of the Cossack girl's shiny green

trousers in its teeth, and they all three pulled – and pulled – and pulled – and sat down with a bump, because the wooden dovecote came up through the hole, and attached to it was the green ground, and out came allotments, and willow trees, and the church with its faded blue dome.

"Look! You see, here we are!" cried the little Cossack girl. They sat in a round green hollow, like the palm of a hand, and the dovecote curved up on one side, and the church dome curved up on the other.

"Is this where my birthday is?" Masha asked the goat kid.

"When, not where," said the kid, flapping its ears. "Between midsummer and midsummer, what have you got?"

"Nothing," said Masha. "Because there's only one midsummer."

"Wrong!" shouted the Cossack girl. "There's the magic time!"

The kid blinked its yellow slotted eyes, and there was a chinking sound exactly like a coin falling into a money box.

"Between the church and the dovecote, what have you got?"

"Nothing," Masha said. "Because you can't see the dovecote and the church dome at the same time."

"Wrong!" the Cossack girl shouted. "There's the enchanted place!"

Kerchink! went the sound of the coin dropping.

But a new, harsh voice croaked, *"Wrong!"* It was a big black crow sitting on the kid's back. *"The proper answer is: Nothing."*

At the bottom of the green hollow was the ice-fisherman's hole. Masha looked through it, and on the other side was a huge white space. No roads, no towns, no trees. It was Nothing. She was tumbling down into it when she felt the Cossack girl's hand seize hold of her own to rescue her.

Chapter 15

Granny had hold of her hand and was patting it gently. "Wake up, little one."

Masha lay blinking at the slanting bars of sunlight peering in between the curtains. It took a moment for the feeling of falling to fade.

"You were dreaming," Granny said.

"Yes, I was." Masha sat up slowly. She wanted to ask her grandmother about the magic time and the enchanted place. But when she opened her mouth, a completely different question came out. "What *was* Mama doing in Turkey?"

Granny turned towards the warm stripes of sunshine. Their clear light on her face made her look very old and tired. "I don't know, Masha."

"But what did Igor say? You've got to tell me," Masha insisted. She grabbed her T-shirt, pulling it roughly over her head, and emerged glaring.

Granny only sighed. "Oh, Mashenka."

"I hate it that no one tells me," said Masha loudly.

"Not even Ma—" She stopped. "I don't suppose even Mama would say," she went on carefully, after a moment. Granny looked so tired, so worried, that Masha desperately wanted to tell her that Mama was all right; she was in Kiev. She was stuck on an island, true; she was being chased by Igor, true; but she was here and she was all right.

She almost blurted it out, but she bit her lip and said nothing.

Granny turned back to her. "Up you get. We've got a lot to do today."

"Have we? What?"

"Why don't you get dressed, and I'll tell you over breakfast."

Granny was already wearing her old faded cotton dress, a headscarf covering up her white hair. But then, as long as Masha had known her, Granny had never bothered to get undressed to go to bed. Masha often thought it must be nice to be old and stop bothering with all those annoying things like having baths, cleaning your teeth, putting on pyjamas and taking them off again. She pulled on her shorts. It was already stickily hot in the flat. Even so, she carefully wound the long Cossack belt round her waist.

Ira made the best breakfasts; this morning it was *syrniky*, little fried cakes of curd cheese, with apricot jam.

"So what have we got to do today?" Masha asked, tucking in next to Gena.

"We're going to the village," said Granny. "Back to my old house to live."

"To the village?" Masha stared. She hadn't been there for a long time. A sudden picture popped into her mind of the dusty road winding through green, green fields, the little low whitewashed houses, the flocks of foolish, officious geese. Oh, how nice to be there, far from anywhere, where it was cool and quiet, and there was nothing to think about except climbing the hill or running down the valley to the river.

But what about Mama?

"We can't go," she said. "We need… I mean…" She stopped. It was so hard not to tell Granny about Mama. But she knew she couldn't just disappear off to the countryside without telling her mother.

"What about your leg, Granny?" she asked instead. "How will we get there?"

"Ira is going to find someone to drive us."

"How long will we stay?"

"We thought for the summer," Ira said, and Masha suddenly remembered what she had said yesterday, that they had to leave. So Ira really was throwing them out.

"The old beekeeper is living in my house," said Granny. "Do you remember him, Masha? There's plenty of room for us too. Wouldn't you like to be back there?"

Masha thought about the dim inside of Granny's house with its hanging bunches of herbs and reeds. She thought about pouring hot wax into water, into the cold hard shapes of nightmares. The village was far, far away from Igor, from Icarus, from everything – and from Mama.

"Yes, I would," she said slowly. "When are we going?"

"This afternoon, if we can find a driver."

"Do we have to go so soon? There's something I have to do here first. Can't we go next week?"

"No. Today or tomorrow." That was Ira. "I think it would be so much better for you in the village," she went on, putting more cakes on Masha's plate. "Don't you?" She sounded pleading.

The village. A blaze of excited hope was kindling in Masha's mind. "Who's going? Will there be room in the car for me and Granny and — and one other person?"

"Who?" Ira asked. "Gena's not going, if that's what you mean."

"No, just — it doesn't matter. I'm only wondering. I mean, I'll be able to stretch out and sleep, won't I?"

"If you want." Ira was still puzzled. "It'll just be you and Granny, and the driver."

"Good," said Masha. "Good!" She knew she wasn't making any sense. She could hardly stop herself grinning. It was going to be all right. She would tell Mama, and they would go *together* to the village, and Igor would never know where they were, never.

"If we go today we'll be in time for the night of Ivana Kupala," said Granny. "How about that? You've never seen a real Ivana Kupala festival, have you, Masha? They've forgotten all about it here in the city. Not in the countryside."

Masha chewed distractedly. She only vaguely knew what Ivana Kupala was. An old Ukrainian festival, something about flowers and fires. Wasn't it … wasn't it … midsummer?

"Is it today?" she demanded.

"Of course. St John's and midsummer's eve."

Masha nearly choked on her mouthful. "But my birthday was on midsummer's eve, and that was almost two weeks ago."

"It's the new calendar," said Gena with the warm pleasure of making a discovery. "Remember, Masha? I looked it up in the encyclopaedia after you asked me. It *is* to do with calendars, like I said. There was an old calendar, and it got a day longer every one hundred and twenty-eight years, because people thought it took the earth three hundred and sixty-five days and six hours to go round the sun in a year. But then they discovered that it actually takes three hundred and sixty-five days, five hours and forty-nine minutes. So the old calendar got all out of sync because the year was just over eleven minutes too long."

He paused, trying to remember the rest. "England and all of Europe changed to a new calendar centuries ago, to bring the year back in line with the sun. But Russia and Ukraine didn't, not until 1917, and by then the old calendar had got a whole thirteen days behind the new one. And the Church here still hasn't changed, so holidays like Christmas and Ivana Kupala are all thirteen days later." He stopped, blushing. They were all staring at him in astonishment.

"What did you say?" asked Ira.

"There was an old calendar that got longer—" he began again patiently.

"Yes, don't repeat it all," his mother cried. "But where on earth did you learn all that?"

"In the encyclopaedia. I told you."

Ira still looked amazed. "Aren't you clever! Why can't you follow up on your schoolwork with the same dedication?"

"But this is interesting," said Gena. "You see, in a way, Masha is right – we have all got two birthdays. According to the new calendar, the one based more accurately on the sun, Masha was born thirteen days ago on midsummer's eve, June … June—"

"June the twenty-third," said Masha impatiently. "Go on."

"But according to the old calendar, it's June the twenty-third and midsummer's eve today. *Happy birthday, dear Masha,*" he sang, *"happy birthday to you!"*

Granny gave an indignant snort. "Newfangled nonsense. You young people believe far too much of what you read in all those books. Ivana Kupala is tonight and always has been."

"Yes, that's what I'm trying to say. It's not that they changed the day; it's just that they changed the way of counting days." Gena broke off. He thought there was no point in trying to explain to an old woman like Babka Praskovia.

But Masha was looking at him with big, shining eyes. "It's today," she breathed. "I found it. So now will I find my heart's desire?"

"You need to be careful of that," said Granny. "Be careful what you wish for on Ivana Kupala."

"Why?"

"Because it might come true, that's why. If you find the magic fern flower." Gena and Masha looked blank. "Don't you learn anything in school?"

"No," they answered in unison.

"What is the magic fern flower?" asked Masha.

"The flower that grants wishes. You must remember the beekeeper's story. He heard it from his grandfather, who heard it from *his* grandfather."

Granny's voice dropped low and mysterious, so that they all leant closer instinctively to listen. "There was an orphan, Petro, who wanted to marry the pretty daughter of the village headman. In our own village it was, Masha. The headman said no, because Petro had no money. So what did the poor love-struck boy do?"

"What?"

"He sold his soul to the devil, that's what. He plucked the magic fern flower that blooms only on the night of Ivana Kupala, and wished for riches. As if money can buy happiness! To find the flower he had to do what the devil told him: murder his own true love's little sister. An innocent child, all for a pot of gold. Much joy he got from it."

"Why, what happened?"

"Went mad, didn't he. Drove his poor lovely wife to misery and distraction. The devil came for him in the end, took him down to hell. And what was left of the gold?"

"What?"

"Nothing. Nothing but a sack of old rubbish."

"That's a true story?" Gena said disbelievingly.

"Oh, you city children." Babka Praskovia took hold of his chin in her strong, gnarled old hand and looked closely into his face. "You don't know a thing, not a blessed thing. You come and stay with me in the village, and I'll tell you stories about Ivana Kupala that'll make your hair stand on end."

"No thanks," said Gena as the old woman let him go. Was Babka Praskovia really a witch? He thought she quite possibly was.

"What a grim tale," Ira commented with a faint shiver. "If the moral's about the evil of riches, perhaps someone should tell it to Igor."

"Oh, he already knows it," Granny said.

"How?" Masha asked, puzzled.

"He grew up with it, like Sveta." Granny was massaging her hurt leg again. "From our village, isn't he. Although he'd rather pretend that he isn't."

Chapter 16

Masha raced along the sunny street past the garages on Gena's rollerblades. She was on her way to let out the goats. The poor goats: who would look after them now? Ira had promised she would find someone.

It was far too hot to hurry, but there were so many things to do. Her mind was in a whirl. She had to get over to the island and tell her mother about going to the village. Masha had planned that Mama would come with them and everything would finally be all right. No one, she had thought, not Igor, not anyone, would be able to find them deep in the countryside, in the whitewashed house at the end of the dusty, unpaved road.

And now it turned out that Igor was from the village too. Masha was furious that she had not known this. When Igor had first appeared in their lives about three years ago, Mama had said he was an old friend. Exactly how old, or where they had met, Masha had never enquired – or perhaps Mama had told her but she had not listened. She hadn't listened, she realized now, because she hadn't wanted to know. She had never liked Igor; even though he had a family of his own, it had always felt as though Mama was somehow trying to replace Papa with him.

Why did Igor have to spoil everything? Now he'd even spoilt Masha's dream of the village as a safe haven. How could Mama have been so stupid as to trust him and let him send her away? And what was this strange power he had over her now, which meant she was hiding on an island talking to herself and wouldn't come home? *If only I knew what happened in Turkey,* Masha thought in a kind of enraged anguish. *If I knew the answers, perhaps everything would be all right. It's like my second birthday, and my present—*

But today was her second birthday! St John's Eve, midsummer's eve. She'd found it. Now she had to find the enchanted place, the spot between the church dome and the dovecote. Because there, she would find her heart's desire.

She thought about Granny's story of Petro the orphan and the magic fern flower, long ago in the village when wishes came true. She didn't want to go mad like that. *Nothing!* she thought she heard again, croaked in a hoarse crow's voice. All the same, she thought, I *am* going to find it. I'm going to find out everything, and then I'll *know.*

"Know!" There was a crow, big and glossy and black, sitting on the fence croaking at her. *"Know!"*

"Oh, shut up." She skidded to a halt and stooped for a pebble to throw. The crow flapped off with derisory slowness.

"Who's throwing stones?" A familiar head popped up behind the fence. "You could damage my church domes. What did you do that for, Masha?"

"Sorry, Fyodor Ivanovich. I didn't mean any harm."

The crow let out a distant cark of laughter.

"Don't do it again. I was looking out for you." Fyodor Ivanovich smiled. "Don't look so alarmed. Are you all set to go and see my sister? I'm about to leave."

Of course, today was Thursday. Masha had completely forgotten her promise. "I can't—"

She suddenly had a wild thought. It came without warning, from the angry turmoil in her mind. She answered before she had time to think about it. "Yes, I'll come. But not to visit your sister and the baby. I want to visit Uncle Igor."

Fyodor Ivanovich looked offended. "Whatever for?"

"Actually, I don't want to see him," she amended. "I want to see Aunt Anya. You know they live close by your sister."

"Of course I know, in Tsarskoe Selo," said the nightwatchman. "All right then. The baby will be disappointed. Just let me wash my hands, and we'll be off."

Masha sat down to wait, and changed the rollerblades for the sandals in her backpack with fingers that trembled with nervous excitement. It was all coming together. Now she'd really know everything. Igor had said he'd be out of town today, so she could ask Anya what had happened to her mother in Turkey. Then Mama wouldn't have to hide any more;

it would be all right; perhaps she'd even be able to help Masha find her second birthday present.

When Fyodor Ivanovich came through the gate, he held his hand out. "Here. I've got something for you."

It was a star, somewhat larger than her open hand, paper-thin and cut from the same soft, shining metal that covered the domes.

"It looks like a sheriff's badge," Masha said.

Fyodor Ivanovich snorted. "It's nothing of the kind. I made them for the dome of our little church down by the river. Remember you asked about it? You gave me the idea. When I've got time I'll put them up, cover it with stars."

"They'll look lovely," said Masha. "And what about the deacon's dovecote?"

"The deacon's..." He gave her a puzzled look. "Wherever did you hear that? I haven't heard it called that for a long time." He watched as Masha tucked the star away carefully in her pocket; it only just fitted, and its points dug gently into her leg. "Ready to go?"

Masha had never walked along the streets of Tsarskoe Selo before; she'd always come in the Mercedes. The enormous brick houses were crowded with fancy turrets and balconies, stuck about with chimneys and galleries, surrounded by smooth naked English lawns and glaring blue swimming pools. They all looked raw: gracelessly new and soullessly unlived-in. Each house and garden lay behind high walls and fences, and outside were piles of sand and bricks, cement mixers, bits of board and planks and broken tiles. Among the debris lounged scrappy stray dogs, and ordinary citizens trudged to and fro on their way to the little old cottages further on, dwarfed by the new mansions and palaces of the rich.

"Are you sure you know what you're doing?" Fyodor Ivanovich asked her. "Thought you weren't too fond of your Uncle Igor."

"I'm not. And he's not my uncle."

"What's he got to do with you and your mother anyway? I understand he found her a job abroad…"

Masha looked up at his lined, honest face, and for a mad moment wondered if she could tell him the whole story. She could actually feel the secrets bulging up like a monstrous balloon inside her, trying to burst out of her mouth.

"I don't know," she said, swallowing hard, and her eyes filled with tears. She looked down, scuffing her toe in the dust. "He wants me to go and live with him."

"You'd have a fine life, I suppose." Fyodor Ivanovich sounded bitter. "A big house, a chauffeur, money and all it can buy. But where does that money come from? That's what I'd like to know. Why does all of it go to them and none of it come to us? I used to have a good job; I used to be paid on time. Now I'm hardly paid at all. And that's because people like your Uncle Igor have stolen everything. Now they run the country according to their own rules. And people like you and me and your mother, we don't matter; we're just there to be used, to do the work while they take the profits."

He seemed to have forgotten she was there as he glared at the new, high walls and spat on the ground in front of them. And then he looked down at her and his face softened, just as Nechipor's had done when he clutched his knife and inveighed against the Turks. "Oh, Masha. So are you going to go and live in the castle there, forget your old friends begging outside the gates?"

"Of course not!" she said indignantly. "I hate Igor. You're right – he's wicked. I've come here to see Aunt Anya, because she's nice, and I need to know – something."

"About your mother, I suppose." Fyodor Ivanovich shook his head. "You be careful. Sometimes it's better not to know."

Masha frowned stubbornly. "No, it isn't."

Fyodor Ivanovich looked worried. But he just said, "I'll be coming back past here in a couple of hours. I'll look out for you, shall I?"

"Thanks, but I don't think I'll be that long." Masha watched as he went round the corner towards his sister's. Then she set off to Igor's house.

Extravagant superstitiousness wasn't Igor's only foible. He also hated animals. He even hated pictures of animals; Masha remembered how unpleasant he'd been about the tiger in her encyclopaedia. It was yet another reason why she loathed him, but it had its useful side – it meant he didn't have a guard dog. As she walked past the other houses, Alsatians and Dobermanns bayed behind the walls and the stray dogs outside jumped up and ran away in stealthy silence. But the drive of Igor's house, when she peeked through the side gate, was quiet and empty. There was no sign of the shining Mercedes or the supercilious driver. Surely that meant Igor wasn't at home.

She stayed looking through the barred gate for a

long time. Nothing moved behind the lace curtains at the windows. Finally she gave the gate a push – but it was locked.

She tried the main gates. Locked too.

She didn't know whether to be relieved or disappointed. She pushed again, and this time to her surprise the gates glided smoothly open under her fingers, silent as the thorn bushes parting at the touch of the hundred-year prince.

Too late, she realized why. The sudden heat on her legs, the low purring, told her. The black Mercedes came to a stop right at her heels. Its back window rolled down and Igor looked out.

"What a pleasant surprise. Move out of the way, there's a good girl, or we'll run you over."

She thought she would have time to edge round the car and run away, but as soon as she was no longer in front of it the Mercedes rolled forward rapidly, grazing her side as it slid past. The gates swung shut behind it and locked.

Igor didn't seem to be very at home in the kitchen. He rummaged impatiently through the cupboards and finally found a packet of biscuits, which he tipped clumsily onto a plate and placed in front of Masha, alongside a glass of juice. Then he lit one of his fat cigars and simply looked at her. There was a long silence.

"Well," he said at last, "aren't you hungry? Go on, eat."

Masha shook her head. Her stomach was clenched with nervousness.

"I was going to come and fetch you later today. That remarkably stubborn old grandmother of yours has changed her mind after all. She's decided to let you come and live here with me."

"She hasn't!"

"Didn't she tell you?" Igor put on his hateful face of mock sadness. "She and that other woman – what's her name? Ira or something – called this morning. They've realized how much better off you'll be here with us. And it gets a tiresome little girl off their hands. They don't want the bother of looking after you any longer. Your grandmother's far too old, and Ira has that boy of hers to keep out of trouble."

"It's not true," said Masha. She was trembling.

"Of course it's true. Your grandmother's going back to the village and wants to leave…" Igor trailed off as his eyes met Masha's stunned gaze.

"How do you know that already?" she whispered.

"About your grandmother going to the village? Of course I know. She doesn't want to take you with her, and I'm sure you don't want to go." His face creased into a grimace of disgust. "Awful, filthy place, full of hideous cows and things."

"It's not true," Masha said again. It was all she could manage. Her mind seemed to have frozen up.

Igor reached over and took the telephone off the side. He placed it on the table in front of her. "Call and ask them. I'll ignore your rudeness for the moment." Masha didn't move. "Go ahead. Call."

Slowly Masha put out her hand towards the telephone. At that moment, it rang. She jumped. Igor seized her outstretched hand, gripping her painfully around the wrist. The phone rang again, insistently.

"Viktor!" Igor shouted. After another couple of rings, the phone fell silent.

Igor released her hand. "Anyway, you've come here by yourself. Why's that, Masha? What do you want?"

"Nothing."

"That's a funny reason to come here. Perhaps you wanted to tell me something. Is that it? Perhaps – where your mother is?"

"No!"

"I think it was. I think—"

There was a soft tap on the kitchen door. Igor hesitated, and then called irritably, "What?"

The door opened, and the driver slid into the room. He bent close to Igor's ear. After a moment or two, Igor gave a nod. "All right. Five minutes." The driver left as quietly as he had entered.

Igor smiled at her suddenly, his wolfish smile. "Never mind. You can tell me later. How about having a look at your new room? Where you'll be living from now on." He stood up and held out a hand to her.

"No, thank you," Masha said.

"Oh, just a quick look, before I drop you off back at the flat to collect your things. Anya's been making it all nice for you: toys, books; she's had new wallpaper put up." He took her hand, gently this time. "You'll like it." He drew her off the chair and towards the door.

"And then do you promise to take me back to the flat?" Masha demanded.

He looked down at her with a hurt expression. "Of course."

The huge house was eerily silent. The thick carpet deadened their footsteps as they climbed the stairs.

Masha was trying desperately to make up her mind. This might be her last chance to find out the truth. She walked with Igor past Anastasia's room and down the long corridor, towards the back of the house. They came to a door at the end.

"Uncle Igor."

Igor stopped, his hand on the doorknob. "What?"

Masha took a deep breath. "I'll tell you where Mama is, if—"

"If what?"

At once Masha knew she'd been incredibly stupid. His face as he looked at her was utterly ruthless.

"I mean, I don't know where she is," she babbled. "But if I knew, I mean, when I know, when I find out, I'll tell you, if—"

"If *what*, little girl?"

"If you tell me what she was doing in Turkey."

Igor opened the door. Sunlight streamed onto the carpet. Dazzled by the brightness, Masha took a hesitant step inside.

"I don't think you really want to know that, and I don't think I'll need you to tell me where she is after all," said Igor. "But I'll keep your offer in mind." He closed the door, shutting her alone inside the room.

"Uncle Igor?" said Masha uncertainly. She heard the click of the key turning in the lock. "Uncle Igor?" There was silence. *"Uncle Igor?"*

Chapter 17

The room was lovely. It was papered in lemon yellow, and full of sunlight. There was a bed with cushions piled on its green and yellow bedspread, a desk with a lamp and a green-painted chair, and, sure enough, many beautiful toys and books, although they were mostly for a child much younger than Masha or Anastasia. Some of them didn't seem to be entirely new either. But everything was clean, expensive, pretty or fun or interesting. Masha flopped down on the bed and stared. This could all be for me, she thought. She imagined having her very own toys like the ones Anastasia had, eating the kind of food that was always in their fridge. Being able to buy everything she wanted. Going to the cinema or the zoo or the fair whenever she liked. Cossack dancing classes. Holidays by the sea. Maybe she'd even be able to go to England to see Alice – why not? Igor had money enough for everything.

And Granny and Ira didn't want her any more.

They thought she should come and live here in the castle with the rich people, and forget all about her old friends. They were the same as her parents after all: her papa who had gone away and left her; her mama who'd liked Igor and his promises more than she'd wanted to stay with Masha. If Igor really wanted to know where Mama was, Masha only had to tell him. Then she could have Anya for a mother. Nice, gentle, sad Anya. And Anastasia for a sister.

Masha choked. She took a deep breath and shrieked again, "Help! Somebody help! I'm locked in!"

Her throat already hurt from screaming. She'd shaken and kicked at the door, pushed at the window so hard she had painful red and blue bruises on her hands. Nothing budged; nobody answered. The great silent house absorbed her cries; they sounded weak and pathetic. The room was almost intolerably warm in the sunshine, and the soft cushions seemed to swallow her up in luxurious comfort. It would be so easy to give in, to curl up on the bed like a pampered cat and fall asleep. She found herself smothering a huge yawn.

But my birthday! she told herself. She had to escape to look for her present. Everyone else had let her down, but there was still the little Cossack girl and the promise of her heart's desire.

A sound came from downstairs. It was the click of a door closing. More soft noises reached her ears: a chair scraping, the thump of something dropped on the floor. Masha felt too scared to scream again. She sat frozen for several minutes before extricating herself from the nest of cushions and tiptoeing over to the door. The keyhole was blocked by the key in the other side, but there was a space beneath the door wide enough to fit her hand up to the wrist. Carefully she lay on the floor and put her eye to the gap. She caught a glimpse of a frilly dress and the end of a pink ribbon as someone entered a room further along the landing.

Masha drew in her breath and bawled, "Nastya!"

Anastasia backed out of her room. Masha couldn't see her top half, just the frills of her skirt, her neat white socks and silver sandals with little flowers on them.

"Who's there?" Anastasia quavered in a scared voice.

"It's me, Masha. I'm locked in."

"Masha?" The silver sandals took a couple of hesitant steps in her direction.

"Is Uncle Igor here?"

"No. I'm on my own. Why are you in the house? Where are you?"

"In the room at the end." Masha banged on the door with her fist. The feet came nearer. "Here. Look down." She fluttered her fingers on the carpet.

"What are you doing in there?" Anastasia sounded outraged. Her knees appeared, then the bunched material of her dress and her long fair hair as she crouched down and peered under the door. Even from the slice of face visible through the gap, Masha could see she was furious. "You've no business being in there. Come out!"

"I can't. I'm locked in. You've got to help me."

Anastasia's one visible eye narrowed. "What do you mean, you're locked in? How did you get in there?"

"Please let me out," Masha begged. "I didn't want to come in here. *Please* unlock the door."

Anastasia knelt up and Masha heard the rattle of the key as she put her hand on it. But she didn't turn it. Instead she said, "You little nosy parker. You were snooping around, weren't you? Serves you right if you got stuck."

"I wasn't snooping!" Now it was Masha's turn to be outraged. "Uncle Igor brought me up to show me the room and then he locked me in—"

"Liar!" said Anastasia. "Papa would never show you this room. I knew you were a liar."

"He did! He said it was going to be my room when I come and live here with you."

Anastasia was silent. Then she said, "That's the stupidest thing I've ever heard. You aren't going to live here and that room's not for anybody."

Masha didn't know what to say. Finally she asked, "Didn't he tell you? About me living here, and him looking for my mama and everything?"

"Who cares where your mama is? As if you could come and live with us." Anastasia's face appeared again in the gap. Her cheeks were red. "I bet you came here to – to steal something. You're just jealous."

"Why would I be jealous of having a father that hits my mother?" Masha snapped. She could have bitten her tongue out a moment later.

"At least I've *got* parents!" Anastasia cried. She jumped up and Masha snatched her fingers out of the way just in time as one of the silver sandals came stamping down. Then they stormed off along the corridor. A door slammed.

Masha rolled over onto her back. How she hated Anastasia, with her frilly dresses and her girly white socks and her boring princess games. She stared at the ceiling, and sighed. Hating her wasn't going to help. It had been stupid to shout like that; now she'd never persuade the other girl to let her out.

"Nastya!" she called. "I'm sorry. I'm really sorry. I didn't mean it. I should never have said that. Nastya!"

The door down the landing opened. Anastasia's sing-song voice came out of it. "Stupid Masha's locked in the ro–om. Stupid Masha's locked in the ro–om…"

Masha stifled a scathing response. Instead she called again, "I'm sorry. Please let me out."

"Bet she really needs the toilet. Bet she really needs the toilet…"

Masha scowled. It was true, and she didn't want to be reminded of the fact. "*Please*. I'll give you whatever you want, or do whatever you want."

"What have you got?"

What could she possibly have that Anastasia didn't have already, and miles better? "Rollerblades," she offered at last. She had Gena's in her backpack.

"Hate rollerblades."

Masha pulled her knees up. She felt something digging into her thigh, and reached into her pocket in puzzlement.

"I know what I've got."

"What?"

"A star. A magic one. It's from a princess."

Anastasia snorted. "As if."

"Look." Masha pushed the star Fyodor Ivanovich had given her under the door. It caught the light from the yellow room and gleamed brilliantly in the dim corridor.

The silver sandals appeared again. Anastasia came down the landing, and before Masha could grab it back she had seized the star. She laughed tauntingly. "It's just an old decoration off ... off a ... a ... from a Christmas tree or something. But thanks anyway." She took a few steps back and sat down, playing with the star in her lap. It shone between her hands with a strange glow of its own, as though still radiating the sun in the yellow room. Anastasia's fingers turned and stroked it dreamily.

"Where's Aunt Anya?" Masha asked at last.

"At the hairdresser's. I was there too but I came back on my own."

"Why?"

"I was sick."

Masha was interested. "Did you twizzle too much on those chairs that spin round?"

"No," said Anastasia, rather too quickly.

"It's just, I did that once. It was awful. I was sick all over the place. It was really embarrassing." Masha's cheeks felt hot just remembering it. "My mother sent me home as well, she was so annoyed."

"Mama didn't send me home. I'm not supposed to go anywhere on my own. But she had all the dye on her hair; if she'd gone out it would probably have turned her head purple or something, so she had to stay. I made her call me a taxi."

"I really like Aunt Anya," said Masha. "She's so pretty."

Anastasia said nothing. Her fingers continued to play with the star. She balanced it on the floor on one point and spun it round. It turned lazily, flashing and glittering.

"I came here to see her," Masha said. "I think she knows what my mama was doing, where Uncle Igor sent her. I thought she might help me."

"What with?" The star fell to the ground, and despite the thick carpet it gave a tiny musical tinkle.

"With finding out what it's all about. Where Mama was, and why she's so scared, and why Igor's chasing her, and where the enchanted place is, and when it's midsummer's eve…"

"It's midsummer's eve today," said Anastasia.

"I know. How do you know?"

"Of course I know. Ivana Kupala. It's the night when you look for the magic fern flower, and if you find it you find your heart's desire."

Yes, of course Anastasia would know. All those fairy-tale games Masha had always thought were so stupid.

"Nastya?"

"Mmm?"

"Please unlock the door. I want to go to my mama. She's in awful trouble and I need to help her."

Anastasia picked up the star and lifted it somewhere out of sight. With a soft rustle of fabric she shuffled along the floor towards the door. "You're so thick, Masha. You're such a baby."

"I just want to get out of here and—"

Anastasia interrupted her. "Get a pen."

"What?"

"Or a hairgrip. No, you wouldn't have one, not with your pathetic haircut. Get a pen from the desk."

"What for?"

"I can't believe you don't know this." Anastasia sounded so superior that Masha wanted to hit her.

"Just get one. It needs to be a ballpoint."

Masha was so confused she couldn't think of a cutting comment. In the end she got up and went over to the desk, where there was a jar full of pens and pencils. "All right, I've got one. What's it for? Why can't you just open the door?"

"Unscrew it and take out the middle bit, the refill."

Again, Masha was so flummoxed that she did as she was told. "OK."

"Now come back to the door."

"And?"

"Use it to poke the key out of the keyhole."

"What for?"

"Duh!" Anastasia began to chant again. "Thicko Masha's stuck in the ro–om…"

"Oh!" Masha couldn't believe she'd been so slow. She knelt and slipped the long narrow refill into the keyhole. After a few moments poking and rattling, the key fell out. Masha lay down again. She could just reach it with her fingertips under the door. She drew it towards her, picked it up, and turned it in the lock.

"Oh well *done*," said Anastasia sarcastically. She was leaning against the wall, still twirling the star between her fingers.

"I'd have thought of it on my own," Masha said heatedly. "Anyway, why should I know how to get out of locked rooms? *My* papa never—" She stopped at the look on Anastasia's face, and took a deep breath. "Thanks," she said. "You saved me."

Anastasia stuck out her tongue. "You got yourself out, all right? I didn't help you." She pointed down the corridor. "Toilet."

Anastasia was waiting for her in the kitchen

afterwards. They both hesitated, staring at each other with odd shyness. Masha had always thought she disliked Anastasia so much, she wasn't sure how to start being nice to her. At last she said, "That room…"

"What about it?"

"It's not really meant for me, is it? Whose is it?"

"My little sister's." Anastasia turned away towards the door.

Masha remembered Igor's words yesterday in the flat. *My wife adores children, and my darling Nastya would love to have a little sister.* "Where is she then?"

"She had cancer," Anastasia said over her shoulder. "Ages ago, before Papa got really rich. The only proper treatment was abroad but my parents couldn't afford to send her."

"You mean – she died?" The other girl didn't answer. "I'm so sorry," Masha said lamely.

"I don't really remember her." Anastasia tossed her head. "And you could never take her place, so don't go thinking you could."

"I'd never think that." Masha followed her out of the kitchen door, remembering she was in a hurry. "I just want my mother back."

She was already through the side gate Anastasia had unlocked when the other girl suddenly took her arm.

"What?"

"I like the star," Anastasia said. "It's my lucky star." She closed the gate between them and ran back towards the house.

Masha stared after her for a moment. But there was no time: she had to run to the bus stop; she had to work out what to do. There was no knowing when Igor would come back and discover she had gone. She couldn't return to Ira's flat and to Granny, because he would look for her there straight away; and anyway, they didn't want her any more: Granny had decided to go to the village without her. She had to find her birthday present; it was today or never. But she could only think of one place left to go, just one safe place that no one had found yet...

At the end of the road a bus came into sight. She sprinted to the stop and hurled herself between the closing doors.

She was going to the island.

Chapter 18

Masha changed back into the rollerblades on the bus. She thought she was going to need them. How could she have been so stupid as to go to Igor's house? She'd lost so much time, and she had an awful feeling she'd said or done something there that had betrayed Mama irretrievably. She'd been so foolishly confident, believing that finding out the truth about her mother would solve all the problems. All that talk of Ivana Kupala and her heart's desire had distracted her into thinking that the whole puzzle was going to unravel to its conclusion, laid out as neatly as the church and the dovecote had arranged themselves in her dream. Oh what an idiot she was!

She sat on the seat as if on prickles, willing the bus to move faster through the sticky heat. There was no one to help her now; nobody wanted her any more. Like Mama, she had to get to the island. She had to hide.

When the bus finally reached her stop she jumped

off and sped towards the market. She wheeled round the corner and was halfway across the road when a great black shape seemed to materialize out of nowhere. Terrified by its suddenness, she flung out her hands to stop herself. They landed on a scorching car bonnet. It was the black Mercedes, and Igor was already emerging from the back door. He fixed her with his livid, ruthless stare, and she felt helpless as a mouse pinned by the hawk's shadow.

"The idea was that your mother would come to you," he said, and though his voice was quiet, Masha knew he was furious. "But I suppose now we'll just have to go to your mother, won't we? Get in the car."

"No," said Masha. It came out as a strange squeak.

Igor's feet were clad in pointed black shoes as mirror-shiny as his car. His sheeny grey trousers had perfect creases in them; his shirtsleeves were fastened with fat gold cufflinks. He smiled at her slowly and absolutely without mirth, a smile which just kept getting wider and wider and more and more full of gold teeth. His hand reached out for her. *Get in the car.*

Masha's feet came to life. With an incredible, satisfying, solid whoosh the wheels on one rollerblade hit the ground and zoomed along it. And the other, whoosh, whoosh, *whoosh!* until she was flying along the pavement beside the fence. She'd never moved so fast in her life. She heard shouting, car doors slamming behind her, the roar of an engine. She didn't look round. The wheels struck the ground and skimmed onwards with fabulous power; the bars of the fence flicked past. And here was the gate to the market. She wheeled through without faltering.

The market was a blur of red and green and yellow.

People, lots and lots of people. She dodged and zig-zagged without for a moment losing speed. Piles of glossy redcurrants, buckets of apricots, stacked bunches of green parsley and dill. A sack of tomatoes – *splat!* There went one under her wheels. Melons! Big yellow rolling globes, and she rolled through them making arcs and wiggles; and here was an old lady with strings of salted dried fish that rattled like dead leaves against her arm as she whizzed past. A string was caught around her elbow – never mind! She shook it off – sorry can't stop – dodge those towers of soap and toilet rolls and *whoa!* Here were eggs, got to be careful, she was speeding off again and – oops, *squish*, there went a pile of juicy red … what? Eugh! Something horrible, guts, big slabs of red flesh and a hot meaty smell like the gates of hell, and here was the butcher's axe glinting down just a hand's breadth from her head, quick-quick and now snip-snap – what was *that?* Mousetraps was what it was, tumbling to the ground and snapping like lots of wicked little jaws, oh *no…*

She burst out of the gate at the other side. Her heart was banging like a hammer in her chest. This street was blissfully empty. No angry stallholders chasing her. No black Mercedes. She wheeled down the road, leaving a trail of squashed food behind her. Someone might notice that. She moved over to the verge. It was harder rollerblading through it, but the grass would hopefully cover her tracks.

She carried on, pushing as hard as she could with her legs, until the market was round the corner and she was among the garages. Then she turned into a lit-tle alley between fences, full of scrubby lilac bushes.

She crawled in among them until she was sure she was out of sight, and then she collapsed.

The heat settled on her like a blanket. Only now, her legs started trembling so much she could hardly unlace the heavy boots.

Masha sat there for a long time. She wasn't really thinking about anything. The heat was a greyish, heavy weight that stifled thought. She watched the dusty lilac leaves, and through them the road that shimmered and baked. The occasional car passed, or rattling buses crammed with people. No Mercedes.

The leaves trembled, and a liver-brown dog pushed its way in beside her. It sniffed at the wheels of the rollerblades and gave them a tentative lick.

"Shh!" Masha whispered. The dog looked at her with calm yellowy eyes and sat down, alert, like a guard dog. She tickled its ears gently, and felt comforted.

Finally she got up. She pulled her sandals out of her backpack and put them on, then set off down to the river carrying the rollerblades. The dog came with her.

Gena was at the bottom of the sandy bank, eating raspberries from bushes that had escaped the allotments.

"Masha! Where've you been?" he said when he saw her. "Mama sent me to find you because you were gone such a long time. What have you been doing?"

"Nothing." Masha felt incredibly tired. She could hardly lift one foot after the other.

"What's up?"

"Nothing."

Gena held out a handful of raspberries. "Well,

anyway, you've got to come back now. Mama's friend is coming round in a couple of hours to take you to the village."

"Didn't you know? I'm not going to the village," Masha said dully. "I can't come back now."

"Why not?"

"There's something I have to do. Two things."

"What things? Can I come too?"

"No." Masha put down the heavy boots. "Thanks for the rollerblades. Look, please tell Ira and – and Granny that I'll be back soon."

"But where shall I tell them you've gone?" Gena frowned. "Masha, where *have* you been? Did you know you're carrying a mousetrap around?"

Masha looked down. Sure enough, a sprung mousetrap dangled from the hem of her T-shirt. She opened it carefully and dropped it on the grass.

"Don't tell them anything," she said. "Don't tell anyone you've seen me. Not anyone. Especially Igor. Promise?"

"All right, I won't tell Igor." Gena was staring at her. "Promise. Is he looking for you?"

"I don't know. Maybe." You can't trust anyone, Masha thought. Ira is throwing me out. She believes Igor. Granny doesn't want me. Even Gena probably thinks I should go and live with Igor.

To be on the safe side, she set off into the allotments, in the opposite direction to the river. Then, when she was out of sight of Gena, she doubled back along a different path leading towards the river and the island. She noticed she'd lost the dog. Feeling lonelier than ever, she walked along the hot, airless path, between grasses tall enough to hide her from prying eyes. The pole of the dovecote was visible on her left, poking into a sky clotting over with dense grey clouds. Ahead, the thin trickle of smoke from the island spooled upwards.

How was she going to get across the water to her mother? Hopefully Nechipor would turn up, as he always did, opportunely. And then perhaps he would come with her in search of his treasure buried in the enchanted place, before it was too late to find her heart's desire.

Chapter 19

Where on earth had Masha been on the rollerblades? Gena wondered. The wheels were completely clogged up with what looked like squashed fruit and eggshells and other less savoury things. He searched around for a stick and sat down to clean them, all the while thinking about what she might be doing now and why she was so worried about Igor and what he was supposed to tell his mother.

He scraped away absently. It was going to be boring here all summer without Masha. She made up such good games. Like this stuff about the trolleybus and the grave and everything. Gena still wasn't sure if he really believed it all. But true or not, it was fun.

Maybe Masha had gone to look for the enchanted place. Wasn't today her special day, her second birth-day? That thing about the calendar was weird. Who would have thought something as mechanically real as the date could turn out to be so arbitrary? Gena felt enormously pleased with the knowledge somehow. It was as if something as solid as the grass and the sky had suddenly shifted, folded up into a piece of paper with a mathematical formula on it. It was just so interesting and satisfying to unravel in your mind.

A dog barked. It was a liver-brown stray, barking and growling furiously at something behind him. Gena looked round. Creeping silently along the sandy track was Igor's sleek Mercedes. It eased imperceptibly to a halt, and a tinted back window rolled down. Igor's head stuck out.

"Hello there, young man," he said jovially. "What are you doing? You look bored."

"Oh, well…" Gena shrugged. His eyes strayed to the long shiny lines of the car. He could see his face mirrored blackly in the door.

His reflection swayed and slid towards him as Igor opened the door and got out. "Want a ride?" he offered. "Move over, give the lad a turn," he said to the driver, who emerged in his mirrored sunglasses smoking a cigarette, as always, and directed at Gena a sinister, eyeless smile.

Gena hesitated.

"You like cars, don't you?" said Igor. "I've seen you admiring mine. Thought you might enjoy a go in the driving seat. See how it feels."

"I would like that," said Gena. He sat down slowly. The seat was bouncy and still warm, and gave off a rich dark smell of leather and smoke. The air in the car was metallic and cool. The dashboard had a walnut veneer and shiny silver fittings, and Igor's array of talismans lined up incongruously along it. Gena found the buttons that slid the windows up and down. The driver silently showed him the air conditioning, the radio and CD player, the thing that squirted water at the windscreen.

"Enough to sell your soul for, eh? I dreamt about having a car like this for years," Igor said tenderly. "It was what I always wanted. No one believed I'd ever be able to buy one. I'll take you for a proper ride one of these days. Out on the highway, show you how fast she can go."

"Oh, yes please," said Gena. "What's this?"

"Compass."

"And this?"

"Horn. No – don't try it."

The driver leant in and gently took Gena's hand away.

"Don't want to go startling the birds," said Igor. "Yes, we'll make a day of it. My Anastasia, and Masha, we'll all go on a trip." He lit a fat cigar and sucked on it thoughtfully. "Does Masha like cars?"

"Not as much as me," said Gena.

"But she'd enjoy a ride, a trip in the country, a picnic? Of course she would. Where is Masha, by the way?"

Gena looked at him pityingly. Did Igor really think a few minutes sitting in his fancy car was going to make him break his promise to Masha?

"I don't know," he said. "I haven't seen her. What does this do?"

"Detects lies from dishonest small boys." Igor puffed out blue smoke. "You must have seen her – how else have you got her rollerblades?"

"They aren't hers; they're mine." Igor was sharp, thought Gena. Scarily sharp. "But yes, actually, she was here. Sorry, I forgot." He climbed out of the coolness of the car, back into the other world of the stuffy afternoon. "Thanks a lot for letting me have a go. It was great."

"My pleasure," said Igor. "Don't forget about that trip. Where did Masha go, do you know?"

"Oh, she didn't say. But I think she went that way." Gena pointed towards the river – the opposite direction to the one he had seen Masha take. "Yeah, that way."

Igor dropped his cigar and lifted a foot to grind it out. *"Yowch!"* he shouted. A little silver object twinkled on the toe of his immaculately shined shoe. Igor had trodden on the mousetrap.

Gena giggled. Then he stopped, although no one had told him to. The driver turned a pair of mirrored sunglasses his way. Igor shook his foot furiously. It should have been funny, but it wasn't. The mousetrap still on his toe, Igor got into the car and slammed the door. The driver followed suit, and the Mercedes started away with an angry spurt of sand. It drove silently down the track which led to the river.

The river was as grey as old metal and all the sunbathers had gone home. Masha sank down, disconsolate, in the hollow where she had found Nechipor with his boat last time. It was empty. She hugged her knees and thought fiercely about nice peaceful *boring* things, about Granny's little cottage with its herby rafters, about picking gooseberries in her garden, about scratching the back of the neighbour's pig with a sharp stick.

It's my second birthday today! she told herself desperately. Something nice has to happen!

It was horribly still. Not a leaf, not a grain of sand

stirred. It felt like the air had turned into some hideous thick woolly jelly – you can't have woolly jelly, Masha told herself sternly. And not a sound. Not one single sound. All the crickets had fallen silent; it was as if the endless thread they had been winding in had knitted itself into a huge grey stuffy jumper and now the whole world was wearing it – you're being very silly, Masha said to herself in Ira's schoolteacher voice. Just sit here and Nechipor will come soon. Of course he will. She wondered if there was something wrong with her ears. Silence blocked them up painfully. She scratched in the sand with her finger, *scratch-scratch*. Oh, thank goodness, she could hear that; she hadn't gone deaf. And now she heard too the soft *pad-pad* of huge paws away in the distance; it was the storm tiger, come to terrify her.

"Hello, Masha," said Igor. He was standing at the edge of the hollow, holding out a hand to her. The driver was beside him, his sunglasses like grey holes in his face. "You've nowhere to run to now, have you? Except the island, and that's where we're all going."

He took her hand and pulled her slowly to her feet. "Come along, it's time."

Pad-pad came the paws, nearer and nearer. A big drop of warm water fell on Masha's cheek. She wasn't sure if it was rain, or if she was crying. She walked slowly up the sand bank, Igor on one side, the driver on the other. The black Mercedes was parked at the top. As Masha looked at it, it went white. The sand was black, the trees were white against an ink-black sky. The tiger opened its mouth and roared.

Out of the roar came something rattling and banging and crashing. It was Icarus the trolleybus, black with livid white stripes, and he drove right *smash* into the back of Igor's Mercedes. The car buckled and howled. The trolleybus door scraped open.

"Next stop, Ivana Kupala," bawled the tinny voice.

"*No!*" Igor shrieked. He was staring at his car in horror.

Bang! came the rain. *Boom!* went the thunder. Masha pulled her hand free, ran forward and jumped through the open door of the trolleybus.

The door crashed closed. There were terrible crunching and groaning noises from the wrecked Mercedes. Icarus shuddered and heaved and with a final huge wrench drove forward into the storm.

Chapter 20

I won't be scared, I won't be scared. Oh no, oh no. Everything is fine – except the Mercedes. Oh yes, oh yes, Masha sang idiotically in her head. Icarus, thank you for saving me. Oh yes, oh yes. (*Crash!*) But, Icarus, where are you taking me? (*Ouch!*) Oh no.

It was more like being in a ship in a storm than a trolleybus. Icarus seemed to lurch up huge waves and smash down the other side of them and roll in the vast furrows in between. Masha pulled herself over to one of the beds. She crouched there, holding on to the frame for dear life and shivering with cold. Icy rain-drops slid from her wet hair under her T-shirt and down her back. The curtains flapped like dim ghosts at the windows. Outside looked as black as night. The lightning illuminated floods of water and – wasn't that a fish?

I won't be scared, I won't be scared, drummed the tune in Masha's head. She dragged out the blanket from beneath her and wrapped herself up in it. It smelt of Granny. Masha closed her eyes so tightly she began to see green and blue lights. And then it all went sickeningly white, because the lightning got even here, inside her eyelids, inside her head.

When her fingers were stiff and aching from clinging to the bed frame, the trolleybus gave an extra-huge jolt and tipped her neatly onto the floor. Luckily the blanket softened her fall, but still, tears of pain started to her eyes. She was so entangled in the blanket she couldn't get up. She rolled helplessly across to the door of the driver's cabin, weeping furiously.

Something hit the window with a *smack!* and stuck there. It seemed to be wet and scaly, and from the middle of it a round, rolling red-veined eye stared in. Below it, a gleam of teeth appeared, grinning. Masha shot out of the blanket and into the driver's cabin, slamming the door behind her. In front, through the wide watery windscreen, all was red. A burning brilliant red. It was raining fire and Icarus was driving right into the heart of it. Masha shut her mouth, closed her ears with her hands and screwed her eyes tight shut, because there was nothing else to do.

And inside her head, this time, it was warmly dark and peaceful. *Dum-dum, dum-dum*, said her blood — at least, she guessed that was what it was. She listened to its comforting rhythm for a while. Her hands slowly uncurled and dropped to her sides; her eyelids gently lifted. Her mouth fell open in wonder.

It wasn't fire at all; it was the loveliest sunset, pink and orange, making her feel warm just looking at it. The sun basked high in it like a great glowing fruit, and its light furred the grass and the trees with gold velvet. Slowly, slowly, Masha backed away and opened the cabin door. The trolleybus stood still, the main door open, inviting her to step outside. The river murmured to itself through the trees. Mingled with it she heard a humming of contented, dreamy voices that floated through the evening air and drew her towards them.

A crowd of people was gathered on the riverbank, building wood into a big bonfire. Others were picking flowers and twisting them into crowns, or tying posies and ribbons to the branches of a young birch. The sun shone through the trees in long level beams; when Masha looked up into them she saw they were full of golden dust whizzing dizzily, silently, out from the warm meadow to the coolness of the river. The whole air was rushing away, and yet the meadow was still and fragrant and the colours of the grass and water were so rich she felt she could almost taste them.

A woman sitting in the grass holding a bunch of flowers turned and saw her. She held out her hand and drew Masha down beside her. The others looked up and murmured friendly greetings. They all seemed to have known her for years and years, because no one asked any questions. One of the women, Masha realized after a while, was her form teacher from school. Over there, on a grey horse whickering softly down its nose, sat Fyodor Ivanovich. And this girl in a white smock, her long hair crowned with flowers, was Anastasia.

Smiling, Anastasia gave her another, half-finished crown, and Masha started to thread in the many flowers, yellow and purple, white and pink and blue, that grew all around.

The evening began to come alive. Insects buzzed and chirred and whirred in the grass; blundering brown-winged beetles zoomed like clumsy aeroplanes. At the river edge the frogs set up their hooting and roaring and creaking. Masha finished off her crown, a fluffy, feathery circlet that smelt of spices and pepper and honey.

"That's right," said the woman who had first greeted her, placing it on Masha's head. Someone else reached down and pushed a boiled egg into her hand. It was Nechipor, grand in a new embroidered shirt.

"Hungry?" he said in his booming voice. "I should think so. I could eat a horse, hooves and all. No offence," he added to the grey horse standing quietly by, Fyodor Ivanovich smiling down from its back. "But a Cossack must think of his stomach, especially when it's as big as mine."

He led Masha over to a large white cloth spread on the grass. There sat Granny, and a lot of other people, making sandwiches of cheese and ham and *salo*, slicing up vegetables and poppy seed buns. She sat and ate, and drank some sweet, fruity drink, and the talk and laughter washed over her like a dim, mysterious, yet comforting wave. The women began to sing, and then gradually they got up from the ground, and they began to dance. The flower crowns turned their heads to angels', to monsters'; their shadows wove long fantastic ribbons through the golden grass. In the twilight under the trees, a fair-haired boy began tuning a violin. At first Masha thought it was Gena, then she wasn't sure. The long notes and chords wavered into tune, achingly sharp and sad.

The sun slipped down, pulling the blanket of the

horizon over its head. The upper air was like warm gingerbread, but a new layer of cool, night-time fragrance flowed up from the ground, tangible as water filling a clear dark glass. Near the river a bright rose bloomed. It was the fire, just coming alight.

Everyone was dancing to music from the violin and an accordion, and the people sang as they circled the fire. Masha watched them, holding hands, now stepping left, now right, bending and swaying like birch trees. The fire burned up, up, until it was a brilliant hot pyramid flinging sparks into the darkening air.

The music swung faster, more lively, sparky and a bit dangerous like the fire. There was more stamping than stepping now in the dance; a rhythm was building with heels and palms. The dancers tossed their heads and put their hands to their hips as the music rocked through them; their faces gleamed hot and red and gold in the flames. The singing was hard and brilliant and at the end of each phrase the women flung high notes like sparks merrily into the air.

And then they dropped down to their heels and the revel really began. Wild, ecstatic Cossack dancing. They crouched and leapt, spun and wheeled in and out of the firelight. Faster, faster, furious, glorious.

"Come on!" said a voice in Masha's ear. She turned and it was her friend, the little Cossack girl. "Come on!" she said again, and together they romped into the whirling, whooping dance.

Calling voices rang out from above on the hillside, where a group of men stood. A wheel of fire suddenly blossomed among them and rolled down the slope, leaving a wavering trail in the grass that flared up and twinkled and then disappeared. A second blazing circle wheeled down, and a third; they rolled to the river and plunged in with a violent hiss. Specks of flame lingered on the water, bending to look at their reflections. The women on the riverbank pulled the flower crowns from their heads and tossed them into the water after the wheels. They floated there, circling idly, and began to drift away downstream.

The fire's voracious roar took on a satisfied purring sound. The music rollicked on, and a shriek of happiness went up from the people. A man and woman holding hands ran and jumped right over the fire. They landed on the other side, hot and laughing, and carried on into the trees.

Another couple jumped over, another. And suddenly everyone was leaping across the flames. Masha found her hand seized by the little Cossack girl. They ran forward, faster; the fire was a hot terrible golden creature lying in wait ahead. Masha jumped and her friend jumped beside her. The fire grabbed at their feet, half playful, half dangerous, and then they had passed right through its heat and flames and were flying down to land on the cool dark other side.

She jumped across again with the boy who had played the violin. The third time she leapt it was by herself alone, to prove she could do it, and she did.

Chapter 21

The fire had died down to its hot embers. The music had finished. People were wandering away, leaving only their voices floating, languid and profound, from the shadowy groves. The sky was dusky but the river seemed to have gathered all the light of the sunset and the fire into it, because it still glowed pink and orange, and the wading bodies of men and women were silhouetted black against it, dipping into liquid fire, liquid sunset.

For a moment, Masha thought she had been left alone. But then the Cossack girl touched her shoulder.

"Let's go, Masha. It's time."

"Time for what?"

"Time to find the enchanted place." It was Nechipor, materializing on her other side. "Are you ready, young fellow – er, lass? Lasses," he added rather doubtfully, surveying the Cossack girl.

"Ready," said Masha.

"Time to find the magic fern flower and your

birthday present, your heart's desire," said her friend. "Are you ready?"

"Ready," said Masha.

They set off together into the dark maze of paths between the allotments.

"Three sets of eyes to look out for three things," said Nechipor. "Cossack number one, look left for the deacon's dovecote. Cossack number two, eyes right for the church dome. And Cossack number three – that's me, in respect of my greater age and experience – will guard the rear for old hairy-legs himself should he take it into his pumpkin head to interfere. Forward march!"

Masha obediently turned her eyes to the left. There was no one in sight, but all around the night was alive with rustling, with whispers and giggles and sighs. The sky still held the milky paleness of midsummer, and the few stars shone faintly. There was a glow of golden-white light ahead of them: the moon was rising.

"I can see the dovecote," Masha whispered. She hadn't meant to whisper – it just came out that way. She tugged on Nechipor's sleeve. "Look!"

And there it was, poking above the trees.

"Well done," boomed Nechipor, clearly not constrained by the mysterious need to whisper. "We'll track down our treasure tonight, you bet we will, by my grandmother's whiskers, God rest her soul. And the devil can just go and stick his head in a sack—"

He broke off rather suddenly. Because the dovecote seemed to have jumped out of the distance and was right in front of them, perched perkily on its one wooden leg. Masha looked more closely. Was that a *chicken's* leg?

A long high cackle of laughter rang out, and the little house, on what definitely *was* a chicken's leg, hopped right round and presented them with a small wooden door. The door popped open, a ladder unfolded with a snap, and skipping down the ladder came a dreadful old lady with a nose curving down and a chin curving up till they almost met like a pair of nutcrackers.

Nechipor's mouth fell open. He even seemed to have turned rather pale. The old woman hobbled rapidly towards them, her knobbly stick tapping busily.

"Good evening! How good of you to come and see me, my dears," she piped in a terribly refined voice. "Oh, how delightful to have guests! Do come and sit down. I don't have cucumber sandwiches to offer you and the tea is a little stronger than you're used to, I expect, but we are so, *so* happy to have you for dinner." And she put one hand politely in front of her mouth and tittered behind it. Then she seized Masha's wrist and in a moment she had dragged all three of them round the dovecote to a long table in a clearing lit by skulls on sticks.

They really were round human skulls on the sticks, with bright torchlight shining out of their eye sockets and between their grinning teeth. The cheerfully ghastly light illuminated the white cloth on the table, which appeared to stretch for ever, spread with a vast array of plates and cups and old-fashioned china teapots. Round the table sat a huge crowd of women. There were old ones and young ones, all with bright lipsticked mouths, thickly plastered eyeshadow and long artificial lashes. They seemed to be having a fantastically good time. They laughed and sang and gossiped and smoked and chomped on huge mouthfuls of food and sipped tea out of dainty china cups holding their little fingers elegantly crooked.

"Ladies," cried the old woman from the dovecote. "Do greet our guests! Just in time for the main course."

All the women turned their heads towards them. Masha had an overwhelming impression of smiling red lips and gleaming teeth and sweeping eyelashes, and somehow she had been whisked into a chair between one slim young woman and one fat old one. The Cossack girl was sitting a little further down, but she couldn't see Nechipor anywhere.

"Oh, you little darling," cooed the thin young woman.

"You little sweetheart," shrieked the old plump one. "But you're so thin, my little dove. Eat! Drink! Plenty of time to fatten you up before the main course."

Together they piled a plate high with dark dripping meat. It looked as if it was raw.

"A drink, my sugarplum," wheedled the young woman, putting a cup of tea in her hand.

Masha took a sip and nearly choked. It wasn't tea at all; it was some thick, treacly liquid with an incredibly salty taste.

Her tormentors cackled with laughter. "It's too strong for her, the little lambkin. Oh, she's so delicious! She's so sweet! A tasty baby girl Cossack!"

Masha defiantly put the cup back to her lips and pretended to drink. Over its rim she looked at the table in growing disbelief. There were rats scampering merrily round the plates and whisking their tails into the cups. From a big pot leapt a pair of long slimy eels, twining in a scaly dance. A rosy piglet came trotting down the tablecloth. It rolled its little eyes at Masha and gave her a sly human smile with human teeth and human lips with red lipstick on them.

Masha dropped the cup. At that moment, there came a roar from further down the table.

"What trickery is this, you bunch of witches? Can't give an honest Cossack a decent glass of *horilka*? Take your witches' brew and tip it right down your scrawny throats till you choke on it, you ugly lot of double-dealing devil's spawn!"

A loud, sarcastic *"Ooh!"* went up from the table. "Angry, is he, our fat red rooster?" screeched someone. "Going to crow for us? Going to strut for us? Go on, give us your best; give us your final display before we pop you in the pot!"

All around the crowd began to thump the handles of their spoons on the table. "Dance! Dance!" they chanted. There was much pushing and shoving among the diners, and then Nechipor was standing on the table, grand and wonderful in his red trousers and embroidered shirt, his moustache bristling and his top-knot swinging as he booted the cups and plates out of the way. *Crash! Tinkle!* The rats fled squeaking as the liquid from the teapots ran into thick, viscous puddles.

"I'll show you stinking, lice-ridden vermin!" roared Nechipor.

Stamp! His boot came down. *Stamp! Stamp!* More plates slid to the ground. Round he went, slowly, round again. He spread his arms wide; his trousers ballooned out like scarlet sails. *Stamp! Stamp!* He bobbed down to his heels, out flashed his legs, his topknot whirled. *Stamp, stamp, stamp-stamp-STAMP—*

And he stopped. Stopped dead, absolutely stuck. As if his boots were nailed to the table, he struggled to lift his feet but could not budge them. His eyes bulged, and his face flushed as darkly red as the spilt puddles from the teapots. A horrible cacophony of laughter rose from the watching crowd. Nechipor grasped one leg with his huge hands and pulled, pulled – and could not move.

"You fiends!" he shouted. "May you be struck blind; may you sink into the ground, you – you monsters… You…"

Oh, how they laughed and laughed. Masha could not bear it. She looked sideways at the little Cossack girl, and her friend looked back. With one accord the two girls jumped up onto the table and ran to join Nechipor. Masha took his right hand, the Cossack girl took his left, and they began to dance.

But it was so hard. Their feet seemed to be weighted with lead. Their limbs dragged; every movement was pushing an impossible weight. All around the air pressed on them, squeezed against them, crushing the breath out of their bodies, the blood out of their veins. And the laughter, the laughter!

A cloud of stinky cheap tobacco smoke wafted into the air.

"Hello, handsome," said a voice Masha knew from somewhere. "Not so jaunty now, are you?"

An old woman draped in a black feather boa stepped up onto the table and pinched Nechipor's bottom familiarly. It was the cigarette dangling from the corner of her mouth, smoked right down to the end, that made Masha recognize her. She was the old woman who had escaped with them from the hospital.

"You too, eh," she said, leering at Masha. "Didn't think I'd see you again so soon. Not enjoying our little party?"

"Not much," said Masha.

"No, well, not really your cup of tea, I suppose." The old woman turned to the crowd. "Anyone got a fag?"

"Boo! Get her off! You're spoiling the show!" they shouted.

"Oh, shut up." The old woman tickled Nechipor's nose with the end of her boa. "Said I'd do you a good turn, didn't I?" she said to Masha. "Guess now's the time. How can I help you?"

"Oh, please, let us go," Masha pleaded. "I've got to find my birthday present."

"A birthday girl, eh? And what's this present then?"

"The magic fern flower," said Masha. "My heart's desire."

The table suddenly went quiet. The woman from the hospital looked sharply down at Masha.

"Oh-ho. It's like *that*, is it? You shouldn't have told me that, young lady. All my sisters are going to want to come with you now."

And indeed the dining crowd were all staring up at her with greedy shining eyes, licking their bright ravenous lips, holding out their hands hungrily.

"Well, you can't," the old woman snapped at them. "I've promised to do a good turn, and I'm going to do it. Off you go then, little bear's paw. Don't get lost, mind. And be careful what you ask for. You know that, don't you? Make the wrong wish and you'll be back here quicker than you expected."

Scarcely believing their good fortune, Masha and the Cossack girl climbed down from the table. But the crowd sent up a screech of dissent.

"You can't do that! Who do you think you are? Boo! Bring back our dinner!"

"What? You won't let me, you old tramps?" screamed the old woman.

"No!" they howled back. "Let the small fry go, but leave us our Cossack, our juicy fat Cossack!"

The old woman twined her feather boa round Nechipor's neck. "Well, I was rather sorry to see you go myself," she drawled to him. "What do you say – time for a game of cards?"

"Yes, cards, cards!" shouted the onlookers, rattling their spoons.

"What, me, a Cossack, play cards with a load of females?" Nechipor bellowed. "Over my dead body!"

"Well now, that's an unwise thing to say." The old woman pulled rather tighter on her boa. Nechipor's eyes goggled. "Come on," she coaxed, stroking his long topknot with a proprietary air. "Just three teeny-weeny little card games, and at the end of it you're free to trot off home to your old melon patch. If you win, that is. But such a fine clever Cossack as yourself will surely beat us poor foolish women, eh?" And she nudged him with her bony thigh.

"And if I lose?" asked Nechipor in a strangled voice.

"If you lose all three games…" She fondled Nechipor's ample stomach and made big eyes at the laughing, clapping crowd. "If you lose, you will be our extra-special, oh-so-honoured guest for dinner."

The crowd burst into a storm of applause and wolf whistles. "Agreed," said Nechipor. "Three games, and you'll be sorry when I beat you hollow."

A grubby, greasy cascade of cards fell out of nowhere and riffled into a pile on the tablecloth. Nechipor took a seat on one side of the table and the old woman sat on the other.

"Nechipor!" cried Masha. "We can't go without you."

"Of course you can," he said. "I'll be right behind you anyway, once I've shown these piggety-faced, maggoty-arsed hags how a real Cossack plays cards. You find the enchanted place, and I'll be there in time to help dig up the treasure."

"Cut along, little girls," said his opponent. "And be quick about it, before we change our minds."

The Cossack girl took Masha's hand and drew her away from the table.

"Well, ladies, what game shall it be?" they heard Nechipor ask in his rumbling voice.

"Devil's poker! Fool! Strip Jack naked!" the crowd shouted, and their cries faded away behind the two girls into the night.

"Do you think he'll be all right?" whispered Masha, clutching her friend's hand tightly.

"Of course he will," she whispered back. "We must be nearly there now, at the enchanted place. Do you recognize it yet?"

The night was silver. A full moon floated in the sky, spilling its ensorcelling light over the trees, the river, the long wet grass that lapped at their legs as they walked wonderingly through it. The whole world was utterly strange in this light, transformed; Masha had never been here before. No one had walked in this undiscovered country; it was just for her.

The dovecote pointed its tall wooden pole into the sky on their left. On the right, the round dome of the church gleamed like a second, duller moon. Nothing stirred, nothing moved. The sky shimmered; only the moonlight endlessly poured down. The enormous night held its breath, Masha held her breath, waiting for something to happen.

Deep in the dark shadows of the trees, a greenish light began to glow. It stretched and swayed like a candle flame, burning brighter and brighter. Slowly Masha pushed her way through the silver grass and the black shadows towards it.

There was a fern, its delicate leaves fringed with moonlight. The green glow came from its heart, from a round bud on a furry stem.

The stem rippled as it grew longer and longer, pushing upwards. At its tip the bud swayed and visibly fattened. As Masha watched in terror and wonder the green shell of the bud split open and curved slowly back. Inside were furled, glowing petals. These soft silky petals stirred as if breathing; they uncurled themselves and stretched and flushed a deeper, brighter colour. The flower opened out, a vivid, shining orange blossom with a fiery heart and black stamens that pointed upwards and trembled.

"The magic fern flower," breathed the little Cossack girl beside her. "Pick it, Masha, and make your wish."

Masha stared at the flower: wide, wide open and glowing. "I can't," she whispered in anguish. It was the most beautiful thing she had ever seen.

"You must!" cried the Cossack girl. "It's your birthday present. It will bring you your heart's desire."

But what *was* her heart's desire? She had to be so careful. She had to be right. This was her only chance, and if she got it wrong she would be captured by the witches, the devil would drive her mad. Oh, if only she knew what she wanted! She could think of nothing, only the flower stood on tiptoe, offering itself, orange and black and burning. She wanted the flower but she knew she couldn't have it. There was nothing in her head but orange and black and burning.

She stretched out her hand and closed her fingers around the living stem. "I wish I could see a Siberian tiger," she said, and she picked the flower.

Chapter 22

At once all the flower's petals crumpled up and withered. They dropped to the ground, one by one, soft and grey and dead. Masha felt a flood of absolute misery fill her up. What had she done? She'd missed her chance; she'd messed it up for ever. She could have asked for anything, *anything*. She could have asked for Igor to leave her and her mother alone, and for everything to be all right. She could have asked for Granny's leg to get better. She could have wished for Nechipor's treasure, or for her own rollerblades. A house to live in. For her father to be returned to her. Anything, but *anything*. And instead she'd made this stupid, stupid wish, this embarrassing, idiotic, moronic wish. She'd ruined everything. She was such a fool! And now the flower was dead and there would never be another one, and she had messed it up. She had failed. It was too awful to cry. It was too awful to do anything but sit in the dirt and hate herself.

And so she sat, looking at nothing, seeing nothing. She wished she was dead.

It was something tickling her palm that made her stir. She couldn't ignore it; it tickled and twisted – eugh, maybe it was some horrible bug—

Full of hate, she lifted her hand, ready to squash what was underneath. But it wasn't a bug. It was a little sprout poking out of the earth. And it was growing as she watched it, almost as the magic flower had done. It put out two little round baby leaves, and a stem. More leaves began to grow, long ones this time, with edges like lions' teeth, growing out in a wheel on the ground. The stems were pinkish and fat and shiny. It was a dandelion. But it grew and grew, a huge dandelion, a monster. Other plants were growing too, thistles and dark violets, and bright green things she didn't recognize, and there was a little whispering, sizzling sound all around; after a moment, she realized it was the sound of the plants growing. Her skin felt damp all over in the sudden warmth. Up grew the plants, up and up into a light green forest that smelt fresh and sappy. The dandelion stems had buds on them, and then they popped out into great bright yellow sunbursts of flowers, as big as her head.

Pad-pad, she heard behind her. Something huge, on velvet paws. And a rumbling and grumbling, like thunder all the way away in … Kamchatka…

She turned her head to see what was behind her. *Pad-pad-pad*. Its paws were huge and furred, with glints of claws embedded in them. Burning orange, striped with black. It was enormous. It looked at Masha with its golden eyes, and its body thrummed and vibrated to an invisible touch.

Hardly daring to breathe, Masha reached up to brush its fur. Her hand looked so small and soft. Under her fingers the harsh fur tingled. Hot and alive, thrumming like a musical instrument to its own unknowable, secret melody. The tiger looked at her with eyes like yellow dandelions. Its huge forehead touched her own. She felt its hot breath, its stink of meat and wildness. Then it stalked past her, moving smooth as silk, heavy as lead in its skin of black and orange. A drift of feathery dandelion seeds settled on its flanks.

It snuffed the air; its tail twitched once, twice, thrice. And then it roared. It roared like the end of the world and tensed all over and bounded away.

The dandelion seeds drifted down in slow silence, silver parachutes the size of her palm, but not big enough to fly away with. She was so tired. The seeds brushed her face with a soft, almost imperceptible touch. Masha curled up in the leaves and closed her eyes.

The last thing she heard was a surprised man's voice saying "Mashenka?" It sounded familiar. She fell asleep before she could answer.

Chapter 23

Birds sang. They sounded small and cheerful. The endless patting and lapping noise was the Dnieper River rocking in its banks. The goats scuffled in the straw and maaed doubtfully. Up above, the trolleybus wires sang their thin, twanging song. And through all those lovely familiar sounds somebody was cataclysmically snoring.

"Sunny," Masha said, "and clear as a bell."

"Just right," said Granny. "Up you get and have a look."

Masha opened her eyes. Between the red and white curtains the sky was a deep, marvellous blue. Blue as Our Lady's gown, as Nechipor would say. The curtains swayed a little in the fresh breeze, their edges rimmed with sunlight.

She was back in her own bed in Icarus the trolleybus. Granny sat by the stove, peeling potatoes. So who was that in the other bed? Someone small and thin, with a tangle of red hair half stuffed under the pillow.

"Mama—?"

"Shh!" said Granny. "Best not wake her yet. Though how she can sleep through that racket…" she added tartly.

The racket came from the floor where, stretched out comfortably, hands clasped on his enormous belly, lay Nechipor. There was something odd and unfamiliar about him, but Masha couldn't work out what. He was snoring fit to wake the dead.

"Run and wash your face, Mashenka, and then you can help me with the potatoes."

Masha obediently got out of bed. She was already wearing her shorts and T-shirt. She stepped over Nechipor and slipped out round the curtain covering the open door.

Icarus was back in his old place under the willow trees, and parked the same way round too, the way he'd always been before all of it had happened. It was a sparkling sunny morning, still fresh and smelling delicious. Masha splashed cold water from the makeshift washstand over her face and flicked some at the goat kid as it wandered up to investigate. "Maaa," it commented, staring sideways at her from a stony yellow eye, but that was all.

Back in the trolleybus she took her place next to Granny and began peeling potatoes. On the floor, Nechipor snorted and heaved. Mama in the bed made little snuffling sounds into the pillow. It all felt very still and quiet and ordinary. Masha found she didn't want to talk about last night. She wanted to just sit in the sunshine with Granny, peeling the potato skins in long curly strips and feeling peaceful.

"Did you find it then, little one?" asked Granny eventually.

Masha nodded.

"And did you make the right wish?"

Masha pondered. She didn't feel any more as if she had done something stupid. Something inside her, something orange and black, purred warmly and strongly. She had done what she could.

"I don't know," she said. Granny patted her hand with her own calloused, brown palm. "Granny?"

"What is it?"

"Would you really have gone away to the village without me?"

"Of course not. Whatever gave you that idea?"

Granny put the potatoes on to boil and began to mix pastry. They sat in companionable silence, listening to the birds and the river. On the floor Nechipor grunted and harrumphed, snorted and sneezed loudly – and woke up.

"Something smells good," he said, his nose twitching as he heaved himself into a sitting position. And Masha finally realized why he looked so odd.

"Nechipor, you've lost your moustache!"

His big fat drooping moustache had been shaved clean off, leaving a defenceless-looking patch of skin beneath his nose. His mouth and chin looked quite different, soft and pale and mushroomy from lack of sun.

Nechipor clapped his hand to his face and stroked the tender place under his nose. "Don't I know, and it isn't half draughty without it," he complained. "Those hideous old hags, may they sleep the rest of their miserable lives in the draught of the devil's own fart – begging your pardon, ladies – till all *their* hair falls out."

"Was it *them*? Those — those witches?" asked Masha. "You didn't lose the card games, did you?"

"Wicked as sin and crooked as Satan himself, the lot of them," he replied, loudly indignant. "What else can you expect from a load of women?"

"Shh!" said Granny. "You'll wake her up."

"Who? Oh…" Nechipor noticed Masha's mother, turning and twisting uneasily in her sleep. An unexpectedly humble, affectionate expression came over his face. "No wonder she's tired," he said in a noisy whisper. "I may as well admit it — I'd still be there in that cursed clearing if it weren't for her."

"Who, Mama?" Masha said, astonished.

"I'd call her my saving angel, except I'm not sure angels play such a mean game of cards. Still," Nechipor added, brightening, "I was only losing because the witches had fed me full of that foul brew they were drinking. A lesser man would have been under the table already. Or rather on it, served up for dinner."

"You mean Mama won the games for you?"

"Those monstrous kin of the devil were cheating outrageously, of course," Nechipor said hastily.

"And no doubt you were too, just not so successfully," Granny put in drily. She leant down, smoothing the coverlet over Masha's mother. "Yes, Sveta always was quite a gambler."

"But how did she get off the island?" Masha wondered. "And how did *I* get back here, come to that?"

"We found you curled up outside the door," said Nechipor. "Perhaps somebody brought you."

"Perhaps." Was it the owner of the man's voice she had heard? That surprised *Mashenka?* she was almost sure she had recognized. But that was something else she didn't want to think about too closely. Better to sit quietly and wait for the potatoes to cook.

"Did you find it then, young fellow – young Masha?" asked Nechipor. "Did you find the enchanted place?"

Once again, Masha nodded.

"And what was there? Did you find the treasure?"

"No treasure, Nechipor. I'm sorry."

Nechipor slapped his huge open palm on the floor. "I might have known! That old slyboots, that flea-bitten, maggoty pile of rabbit droppings, thought he could trick a pair of honest Cossacks, did he? May his nose be covered in warts, his toes go mouldy, and may *I* be afflicted with eternal bellyache if I ever fall for his tricks again!"

"Shh!" Granny said. "Anyway, you should have known better than to go looking for treasure on the night of Ivana Kupala."

"You're right." Nechipor sighed gustily and clambered to his feet. "I'd better get back to the only treasure I have got – my melon patch. Who knows what's left there after last night's shenanigans."

"Oh, must you go?" Masha's face fell.

Standing, the Cossack's topknot almost brushed the trolleybus ceiling. He towered there for a moment, smiling down at her. "Cheer up! Remember, you're an honorary Cossack. High of heart, we are, and scared of nothing, not even old goat-foot himself and all his wicked minions. You take good care of that mother of yours. Come and visit my field in a couple of weeks. My melons will be fatter than me by then, and I'll be able to offer you the sweetest, juiciest slice this side of Mirgorod."

"All right." Masha smiled back. "I'll bring Mama."

"You do that." Nechipor swept her and Granny a deep bow, and then he had vanished through the doorway.

The potatoes were ready. Masha added butter and seasoning, while Granny rolled the pastry into long sausages which she then sliced into rounds. Together they filled them with mashed potato and pinched the pastry edges together to make *vareniky*. The dumplings were nearly cooked, floating to the top of the pan of boiling water, before Mama woke. She sat up, her hair sticking out comically round her pale, sleep-crumpled face, and held out her arms. Masha ran into them.

Mama didn't want to talk either. She sat rocking slightly, letting Masha on her knee untangle the knots of hair with her fingers.

Granny put the *vareniky*, mixed with crispy slices of fried onion, into a huge clay pot to keep warm. "Your favourite," she said to Mama gently.

Mama gave her a wan smile. "I used to dream about your potato *vareniky*, when I was locked up with not enough to eat in Turkey. And on the island too. I got so tired of fish soup over there; I hope I never eat it again as long as I live."

"How did you get off the island?" Masha asked, picking a last bedraggled dandelion seed – what was that doing there? – out of Mama's hair and smoothing the strands down tidily for her.

"So many strange things happened last night, I don't know which were real and which were just dreams," her mother said reluctantly. "Perhaps it's better not to talk about it. I thought I went for a ride in this trolleybus, and then I was playing cards somewhere in the woods … I thought I saw all sorts of things. I thought I saw Igor being chased by a tiger, for instance. Have I got a temperature, Granny?" she asked suddenly, sounding just like a little girl.

Granny put a soothing hand on her forehead. "Better lie down, sweetheart," she said in the loving voice she usually reserved for Masha, and Masha felt a sudden odd jab of jealousy.

Mama leant back against the pillows. "I shouldn't be here at all, but I haven't got the strength to run away again," she said faintly.

Granny served the *vareniky* and poured them all cups of fragrant herbal tea. Mama lay propped on the pillows, staring at the blue sky through the window with a strange, blank, hopeless expression Masha didn't like to look at. How odd that they were sitting here quietly, like on any summer's day when there was nothing to do except eat lunch. Outside, the willow leaves rustled. The goat kid made funny small noises to itself and started nibbling the door curtain.

Then there were footsteps slipping and sliding in the sand, and a voice shouting, "Masha! Babka Praskovia!"

Mama sat bolt upright with a look of panic on her face. But Masha said, "It's all right – it's Gena."

A moment later, Gena's puzzled face appeared in the doorway. "Has something happened to your trolleybus?" he asked uncertainly. "Something about the door…"

"It's turned round again, of course!" crowed Masha, clapping her hands. "There was another thunderstorm yesterday, remember?"

Gena frowned, and then dismissed this. He had

more important things to say. "You won't believe what's happened. Mama's on her way to tell you but I ran ahead. She's had this most incredible phone call from Igor."

"Igor?" cried Masha's mother, and Gena noticed her for the first time. He goggled, but went on with his news.

"Do you know what he said? Mama reckons he's gone mad. He was crying and going on about what a terrible man he is, and he said he was attacked by a tiger and he's nearly dead."

He watched the reaction to his news. It seemed a bit unsatisfactory. No one fell off their chair, or shrieked with amazement. Masha's mother, under that weird new hairstyle, had gone awfully pale; Masha was looking almost angry, for some reason. Babka Praskovia only nodded slowly.

"He's got to be barmy," said Gena, a bit less confidently. "You know, Mama actually phoned the zoo afterwards, she was that curious. But they said they hadn't lost any tigers."

"Perhaps Igor was in the zoo looking for them," said Masha. She knew perfectly well that wasn't true. She knew which tiger had nearly killed Igor.

"Hello?" called a voice. Ira knocked on the side of the trolleybus before pulling open the curtain. She looked round at the scene inside with her mouth open. "Sveta? Sveta, is that you?"

"Hello, Ira," Masha's mother whispered.

Ira hesitated for a moment. Then she jumped into the trolleybus and threw her arms round her friend. "Sveta darling, where have you been? What have you done to yourself? Svetochka…"

Mama didn't answer.

"Tell them about Igor." Gena was impatient with all this hugging and crying. "You won't believe it," he said to the trolleybus in general. "Mama didn't. He's gone nuts. Completely bonkers. He's lost his marbles."

Masha remembered her grandmother's story, about the man who had gone mad after Ivana Kupala. A cold shiver tiptoed along her spine.

"He said to tell you he was sorry," Ira said to Masha's mother. "Sveta, what have you been doing all this time? What's been going on with Igor?"

"Don't ask." Mama sat up, listening. "Oh, who's that?" she wailed.

A vehicle was approaching, rattling and wheezing. It crashed to a halt outside the trolleybus.

Masha knelt up on the bed and looked out of the window. There stood a strange, ghostly car. It was painted a particularly unpleasant shade of dull, dirty white. The front was all right, but the back was smashed in as if it were made of paper. The engine spluttered and fell silent, and a man got out. He was small and balding, with an unassuming, forgettable face. He cleared his throat nervously, eyeing the trolleybus as if it were a large and unpredictable animal.

Gena pulled aside the door curtain curiously, and Masha joined him in the doorway. The man stared at them, and they stared back. Neither of the children recognized him.

"Got a message," mumbled the man at last. "For someone called Sveta." He held out a very fat envelope.

"Sveta who? There's no one called Sveta here," said Masha instantly.

Behind them Ira asked, "Who are you?"

"It's the driver," said Gena in amazement.

"What driver?"

"Aren't you?" Gena went on to the man. "Uncle Igor's driver? And that's his car. What on earth has happened to it? Why's it changed colour?" Gena was rather upset to see the state of the beautiful Mercedes. It was unrecognizable. He had only realized what it was from the icons jumbled up along the dashboard, the furry paw and the prayer beads still dangling absurdly from the mirror. And he only knew it was the driver because he had come with the car. Without his sunglasses he looked utterly ordinary and unthreatening. Gena realized he had never even heard him speak before.

"What happened to it? Ask your little girlfriend," answered the man.

Gena was too surprised to be offended by him calling Masha his girlfriend. And Masha wasn't listening. She was peering into the car.

"Is that Igor in there?" she asked.

The windows of the Mercedes seemed to have lost some of their tinting. They were a foggy grey now, and behind them a figure was visible, hunched up on the back seat. Masha pushed past Gena and walked over to the car. She bent and looked right in the window. She looked for a long time. Then she turned round, took the envelope from the driver's hand, and stepped back into the trolleybus. She went straight over and gave the envelope to her mother.

The driver got back in the hideous car and it drove away, lurching and groaning, through the clinging sand.

Ira stared at Masha's mother, her face full of speechless surmise. Then she shook herself and said briskly,

"Well, we should leave you to your lunch. Come along, Gena."

"Oh, but—" Gena was bursting with questions. What was in the envelope? What had Masha seen in the back of the car? What had *happened*, for goodness' sake? But Ira, after kissing Sveta, put her hand on his shoulder and steered him firmly out of the door.

Envelopes! That reminded him. "Wait a minute," he said, rummaging in his pocket for a thin and rather crumpled envelope. "I've got a letter for you, Masha."

He wanted to tell her more but Ira took the letter and laid it on the bed next to Masha before stepping out into the sunshine. "Come on, Gena. It's such a lovely day. How about a stroll down to the river?"

"Oh, all right." Gena suddenly brightened. "We might meet Nechipor."

"Nechipor? That's a name you don't often hear these days. Whoever do you mean?"

Ira and Gena set off into the maze of paths that led through the allotments.

"He's got a topknot and a moustache and bright red trousers…"

"Oh, another of your and Masha's Cossack games," Ira said tolerantly as they walked on.

Slightly jealous, Masha watched their heads bobbing along above the bushes. Then the bushes got too high. The branches trembled and whispered, further, further away. There was a sudden flash of colour: a patch of bright red between the green leaves.

"…a friend of Masha's," a voice floated back. "A real, honest-to-God Cossack!"

Chapter 24

Masha sat cross-legged on the riverbank. It was late afternoon; the low sun that lent the oak trees on the island a brief glamour beamed warm on her cheek. In her lap lay the encyclopaedia of animals and the letter Gena had given her.

She closed her eyes and looked at the glowing inside of her eyelids. Orange, striped with black. She thought about the tiger. And she thought about how the tiger must have looked to Igor.

"It must have been a rival mafia gang," her mother had said. "They do things like this to each other. He can't have paid them off properly. Yes, that's it. Or perhaps it was that long-suffering wife of his," she had said. "Maybe she finally had enough."

Her mother would not let Masha read the letter inside the fat envelope the driver had brought.

"Then at least tell me what it says," Masha demanded. "Tell me why he sent all this."

All this was money. The envelope was so fat

because it was stuffed full of hundred-dollar bills. They bulged out of the envelope and fell onto the bed and the floor of the trolleybus.

"Because he's sorry," said her mother. "He says. And this – these are my wages. The money I earned when I was forced to work in Turkey."

"It's Nechipor's treasure," Masha said. She had thought treasure was always gold, strings of pearls, crowns crusted with diamonds. But she supposed money would do as well.

"He says we're safe; that he won't make me go back; that he'll never harm us," her mama said. She looked blankly at all the money scattered around her, and held out her arms to Masha. "Come and give me a hug, my love. I'm never going away again."

"None of it has happened like I thought," Masha said later to Granny, while Mama was outside.

"It never does," Granny answered. Her leg was still propped on a stool: that was one thing that hadn't changed.

"Does it hurt much? I'm sorry I didn't wish for it to get better."

"It'll get better anyway," said Granny. "You can't wish for everything. You did a good job, Mashenka."

But I never meant most of it, Masha thought now, sitting in the fiery glow of her closed eyelids with the sun behind them. And I never found out about Mama and Igor. Perhaps it doesn't matter any more.

The orange glow went dark as a shadow fell across her.

"Hello, sleepyhead."

Masha opened her eyes and had to blink a lot, dazzled. It was Fyodor Ivanovich.

"Hello," she said. "Where's your horse?"

Fyodor Ivanovich looked puzzled. He countered, "Where are your rollerblades?"

"They aren't mine. I only borrowed them."

"We got some new work in at the garage today," Fyodor Ivanovich said. "A car that's had some *very* strange things happen to it. Needs a paint job, as well as some major straightening out. And it was a nice Mercedes once." He gave Masha a quizzical glance. "But I'm on my way to the church first. Look." He unfolded a flat paper-wrapped package, and held out a heap of sparkling stars.

"I gave mine away," Masha said. "I hope you don't mind."

"Of course not. So long as whoever you gave it to deserved it."

"I think so."

Fyodor Ivanovich wrapped the gleaming handful up again. "So you're home in your trolleybus. Saw you and your granny there this morning. Nice to be back?"

Masha nodded. "And my mama has come home too," she said. "For good."

"Well, there's good news! So now you've got everything you want, have you?"

"Nearly." Masha waved as he set off along the riverbank. "I haven't got my own rollerblades," she called after him.

"I should hope not," said another voice. Masha jumped. "You children, you want the world – you're spoilt. That's what you are, spoilt!"

Masha stared. A shabby old woman pulling a cart on pram wheels had appeared out of nowhere. She had lost her feather boa but she still had the cigarette glued to her lower lip.

"No empty bottles, ducky?" she wheedled, rattling the empty beer and fizzy drink bottles in the cart, which could be returned to the factories for a few coins. "Or how about ten kopeks for a hungry old grandmother, eh?"

Masha drank the last of the lemonade she'd brought with her and handed over the empty bottle. "Here you are."

The old woman inspected it with a disappointed air before wedging it into her cart. "Looks like Ivana Kupala didn't bring you much to share. What's the matter: don't like what you asked for?"

"It's a trick really," said Masha. "That's why in stories people always make the wrong wish. You think it's all about knowing, but I don't think you can know your heart's desire; or, you can never know what it will do."

"What were you expecting?" asked the woman, sucking on her cigarette butt. "I told you – you're spoilt. Think you can have everything. You should count yourself lucky, Mistress Masha. You're still here; I'm not taking you along with me, much as I'd like to." And she suddenly reached down, seized Masha's cheek and squeezed it. "But maybe I'll come back for you, one of these days." She grinned, her dirty, leathery face close to Masha's for a moment. Then she walked away down the bank, her little cart clattering and tinkling along behind her.

Masha looked around nervously to see who else might pop up to startle her. There was one other person she was almost expecting. But the riverbank was deserted in the drowsy late sun. She closed her eyes again, listening. She was waiting for someone to say her name. Rustling leaves, crickets whirring, and that was all. She was half sorry, half relieved. She wasn't sure she had recognized that voice anyway. She wasn't sure that if he were to come along right now, she would recognize him. Perhaps the old woman was right: she wanted too much. Getting one parent back was good enough.

So she looked at the things in her lap. First, the encyclopaedia of animals Anya had given her, where the Siberian tiger had been. Masha wondered if that page was blank now. She wondered where the tiger was, after what it had done. Had it gone back to Kamchatka; back to the same place that voice had come from? She didn't know what to do with the book. Would she ever dare open it again? She weighed it experimentally in her hand, and then on a sudden impulse she threw it into the river. It landed *smack!* on its back on the water and floated, slowly slipping away downstream.

Second, the envelope Gena had given her. It said *Masha* on it in big round English letters, with a smiley face inside the first *a* and a flower sprouting from the tail of the second. Inside were a letter and a photograph.

Masha looked at these. And then she jumped up, kicked off her sandals and ran down the riverbank to where the encyclopaedia was gliding away. She waded out into the cool water to retrieve it. Its hard shiny cover seemed to have kept it from much harm.

She returned to her place and propped the book open beside her on the grass to dry. Then she turned her attention back to the letter. It was written in English, and said:

Dear Masha,

Hello! I have heard lots about you from Gena; I know you live in a trolleybus (although I don't really know what a trolleybus is; we don't have them in England). And I know you can dance really well, and to show you that I do know a bit about Cossacks I have sent you a photo.

Yes, this is me! I am coming to Ukraine soon – my dad has got some work in Kiev and he is bringing me and my mum for a holiday.

So we will get to meet each other. I've been reading and dreaming lots about Ukraine and I'm really looking forward to it.

See you soon!

From Alice

Masha couldn't read English very well, but she could understand most of this letter. It also had pictures drawn down both margins. On the left there were knights on horses with swords and shields, some fish, and an animal Masha thought might be the mysterious guinea pig. On the other side there were people in Cossack costumes jumping over a big fire. There was also a small house standing on a chicken's leg, and a curly fern plant with a big flower sprouting out of it.

The photograph showed a girl Masha's age, peeking out from under a furry Cossack hat. Her Cossack trousers were green and shiny, her boots were red as cherries, and round her waist was a red and orange woven belt just like the one Masha had tied round her waist.

Masha smiled into the sun. She beamed at the gilded oak trees on the island. She put the letter and photograph back in the envelope, and slipped it inside the animal encyclopaedia. She had decided she would never dare look at that book again, but now she thought she would probably want to show it to her friend, the little Cossack girl.

The book of animals tucked under her arm, Masha set off for home.

Glossary

borscht beetroot soup

Cossacks runaway serfs and soldiers who founded their own society and army on the Ukrainian and Russian steppes in the seventeenth century. They battled the Poles and the Turks and Crimean Tatars before losing their independence to the Russian Empire. Their songs, dances, costumes and history are still a beloved part of Ukrainian tradition

dacha summer cottage

hopak a Cossack dance

horilka vodka

rusalka a female river spirit

salo salted pork fat, a Ukrainian delicacy

samogon home-made vodka

shashlik kebab

syrniky small fried curd cheese cakes

vareniky dumplings filled with potatoes, cabbage, fruit or curd cheese

NOTE ON IVANA KUPALA

An ancient Slavic midsummer festival. Originally a pagan celebration (where the word Kupala comes from) it was later combined with the Christian feast of St John the Baptist (Ivan). On the night of Ivana Kupala people lit bonfires and jumped through the flames; if a couple managed to hold hands as they jumped it meant they would stay together for a long time. Girls floated candles and flower wreaths on the river to foretell who they would marry. Midnight on the eve of Ivana Kupala was the only time the fern flower bloomed. It was said to grant wishes and bring riches but only if the seeker could withstand the devil and evil spirits. One of the most famous retellings of the fern flower legend is *The Eve of Ivana Kupala* by Nikolai Gogol, and this is the story Granny tells in chapter fifteen.

Amnesty International

Amnesty International is a movement of ordinary people from across the world standing up for humanity and human rights. Our purpose is to protect individuals wherever justice, fairness, freedom and truth are denied.

Human rights are basic principles that allow individuals the freedom to live dignified lives, free from abuse, fear and want, and free to express their own beliefs. Human rights belong to all of us, regardless of who we are or where we live.

We work in two main ways: we try to make people aware of human rights and we oppose abuses of human rights.

Youth Groups
We have an active membership of over 550 youth groups. Youth groups are gatherings of young people in schools, sixth form colleges or youth clubs who meet to campaign for Amnesty International. They hold publicity stunts, write letters to government leaders and officials, fundraise, get publicity in their local paper, hold assemblies and create displays. You can also join as an individual member and receive magazines and letter-writing actions.

If you would like to join Amnesty International or set up a youth group, or simply find out more, please telephone our Education and Student Team on 020 7033 1596, email student@amnesty.org.uk or visit our website.

Amnesty International UK, The Human Rights Action Centre, 17–25 New Inn Yard, London EC2A 3EA. Tel: 020 7033 1500.

www.amnesty.org.uk

"It is difficult to explain how greatly our life changed after that first postcard. I never felt lonely any more... Every letter was a miracle – they changed my life, they gave me hope. And I think the correspondence saved my mother from having a nervous breakdown or from total despair."

Marina Aidova, who was eight years old when her father was arrested and imprisoned by the Soviet authorities. Amnesty International asked its members to write to Marina and her mother Lera.

"Amnesty's greetings cards really helped me in prison. In total, I received more than 4,000 – amazing! I read each one: the best, I think, were those from children and other student activists... It amazed me to see that those children know about human rights. What a good omen for the future!"

Ignatius Mahendra Kusuma Wardhana, an Indonesian student who was arrested at a peaceful demonstration in 2003 and spent more than two years behind bars, where he was beaten and threatened.

"It is impossible to paint an accurate picture of [my] reactions as I sat in that tiny cell, the floor carpeted with cards and envelopes, generated through Amnesty's efforts. It was deeply touching, greatly encouraging and strengthening... I knew that I was not alone... Maybe you just send one card – but all of these cards are like little drops of water that combine to create an avalanche of pressure... It was so moving. I gained such strength from them. I knew I had committed no crime and now I knew the world also knew why I was in prison."

Chris Anyanwu, *Nigerian journalist and Amnesty International prisoner of conscience, imprisoned in 1995 and released in 1998. Nine thousand cards were delivered.*

It was meant to be like coming home. All her life, Safi's parents have dreamt of returning to Grandpa's native village in Crimea. But exchanging their sunny Uzbek house for a squalid camp is more like a nightmare. Will the return to a country where no one welcomes them tear Safi's family apart, or can this strange land ever become home?

A compelling story about the Crimean Tatars' struggle to reclaim the land from which they were exiled in the Second World War.

Oscar Martin was fourteen when he vanished from his Iowa farmhouse home in June 1914. His sister said that Oscar rowed out to sea, but there are no oceans in Iowa – so how was that possible?

Nearly a century later, Lucy Martin and her parents move to that same farmhouse, where her father also mysteriously disappears. When she finds the magical Book of Story Beginnings, Oscar reappears and together they set out into a fantastic dream-like world in search of a happy ending.